NIGHT SHELTER

BY THE SAME AUTHOR

FICTION

A Smell of Fraud
The Predators
Caring for Cathy
Blue Lantern
Present Tense
The Cruel Peak
Codename Wolf
Don't Cry for the Brave
The Unforgiving Shore
Rendezvous with Death

NON-FICTION

Teaching Yourself Tranquillity
The Happy Humanist

gilhogg.co.uk

Matador
9 Priory Business Park,
Wistow Road, Kibworth Beauchamp,
Leicestershire. LE8 0RX
Tel: 0116 279 2299
Email: books@troubador.co.uk
Web: www.troubador.co.uk/matador
Twitter: @matadorbooks

ISBN 978 1788033 633

British Library Cataloguing in Publication Data.
A catalogue record for this book is available from the British Library.

Printed and bound in the UK by TJ International, Padstow, Cornwall
Typeset in 12pt Bembo by Troubador Publishing Ltd, Leicester, UK

Matador is an imprint of Troubador Publishing Ltd

To my wife, Maureen
Regards,
Gil

1

A fire lit the derelict building site behind St Edith's Night Shelter for the homeless. The vagrants, abandoning the warmth of the flames, had started to queue for supper. The line was orderly, extending from the fireside, across the yard to the serving table inside the door of the shelter. Nobody was overly drunk or stoned. The flames flickered on the waiting figures, distorting them into the bent and the sinister.

Jimmy Morton watched from the dark outskirts as the line diminished; the diners now settled on the plank seats inside the shelter with their meal. It was a clear, icy night. He felt cold. He was about to collect the helping of food put aside for him and take it upstairs to his room, when he saw an old woman swaddled in an overcoat, with a scarf over her hair, picking her way through the litter toward the shelter. He recognised her and anticipated that she was looking for him.

"Jimmy!" she breathed loudly when she was a few yards away.

"Whatcha, Betty?"

She came close and put her hand on his arm. "Come over to the flat, willya?" she croaked.

"I'm workin'."

"I need y'help. Urgent!" Her voice was shaky.

"Wassup?"

She looked round fearfully. The tail of the queue had disappeared indoors. "Please, Jimmy!"

Her alarm affected him without the need for more words. Betty Thrussell was a person with a lot of troubles. "Hang on a minit," he said. He went across to the shelter, pushed through the crowd around the stewpots to find Paul Emmett. "Hey Paul, Betty Thrussell, my old landlady, has a problem. Wants me to go over there…"

Paul didn't speak. He raised the palms of his hands and turned down the corners of his mouth. 'What do I care?' was the signal.

Jimmy followed Betty Thrussell across the yard to the tenements on Butchers' Row. They felt their way into the ill-lit entrance to the building, found the stairs and climbed two floors in the urine stink to Betty's flat. She unlocked the door and let him in, her chest heaving with distress.

The solitary unshaded bulb in the hall illuminated the body of a young woman with red and green coloured hair in a skimpy, silvery-transparent dress. She was lying on her side on a mangy rug.

"Hell! It's Eva. Wassa matter with her?" He bent down over the body, staring but not touching. The bare, chalky arms, parchment face and eye slits with the whites showing answered his question. "Jeez, Betty, she looks to me like dead. Wotappened?"

"I dunno. I found 'er here. I just come back from the pub wiv a headache. Now I got me a real headache. You know 'er, Jimmy?"

"Course I know 'er."

"One of Johan's girls. I seener." Betty nodded. She'd heard the talk.

So had Jimmy. Johan Tomachek ran a brothel from his flat along the corridor. Jimmy knew Eva slightly as a presence in Harry's Café on the corner and seeing her around the streets. She was – or had been – a lively and attractive Polish girl, worn down by her dope-master relationship with Johan. Jimmy had bought Eva a cup of coffee at the café on two, three occasions at most. Eva had told him she was nineteen but she had looked older, hollow eyed, pallid, with creases on her forehead. She had been well-shaped but her sexual attractions were draining away – and now her life had drained away.

He also knew Johan enough to greet and say a word about the weather. Jimmy imagined the hell that Eva had been in. She had only spoken a little in Harry's Café. She never approached him as a john. She had been looking for somebody – anybody – who would find a way out for her. She couldn't seem to do it on her own. Apart from sharing a drink and a cheery word, Jimmy had kept clear instinctively. She had been trouble, double trouble in that Johan regarded her as his property.

"Help me to get her out of here, Jimmy," Betty whined.

"We oughta call the cops. Where's Kevin?"

Kevin was Betty's eighteen-year-old son.

"I dunno where. He ain't been in here in the last coupla weeks."

"Well, who dumped Eva here?"

"I dunno. I swear, Jimmy."

"Nobody else here but you. *Must* be Kevin."

Kevin lived nobody knew quite where. He slept around with his chics. But he visited his mum occasionally and slipped her a few quid. "He must have left her here after..."

"Don't get him innit, please, Jimmy," Betty squealed.

"Looks like he's already involved."

"Don't say that. You don't know. Help me. Let's get her out. Please, Jimmy."

"This is Kevin's problem, Betty."

"I don't want nothin' to do with the cops, nor does he."

"Neither do I."

Jimmy opened the door and looked up and down the dingy, deserted corridor. He went out and walked along past the damp walls with their cracked and flaking plaster, toward Johan's flat. The door was shut. He hesitated to ring the bell. He was thinking what to do. He went back to Betty's flat. He could have picked up the light body of Eva in his arms and carried her to Johan's doorway in seconds, but he decided he wasn't going to do that.

"You're asking more than I can do, Betty," he said when he returned to her. "If I touch that body…"

"Nobody will know."

"Oh, yeah they will. These homicide boys are smart an' they got all the technology."

"Oh, Jimmy, what's goin' to 'appen?"

"You'll make it worse if you don't call 'em, Betty. Worse for you. Worse for Kevin if he's innit."

Betty Thrussell had been good to Jimmy. She gave him a home after his mother died. He couldn't forget that. But he was firm. She was crying and he felt sorry for her. All his life he'd been around violence and crime; it was part of the scene in which he had lived, in the streets, the shops, the pubs and in the homes. He had learned that when you came anywhere near a crime, you had to be able to show you weren't involved.

"Get Kevin. He must be around. Eva can't have been here long. He's not going to leave 'er 'ere."

"Don't let me be alone wiv 'er."

"When are you movin'?"

"I ain't. Let the buggers throw me out!"

"Haven't you been offered a place?"

"Nah. I'm a squatter, they say. They'll just kick me out. I'll probably end up across the patch at the shelter."

"I gotta get back to work, Betty."

He left her reluctantly but certain about what he was doing.

When Jimmy reached the entrance to the tenements downstairs, he recognised the stocky figure of Kevin Thrussell bustling through the swing door. Kevin was three years younger than him, but he had a steely, adult poise. They had both lived in the same house, the Thrussell flat, for a few years until Jimmy got a live-in job as a cleaner at St Edith's. They weren't enemies nor were they friends. There was always a hint of suspicion and disagreement between them. He couldn't avoid Kevin at this moment, although he wished to. He couldn't walk past him pretending not to know him in the poor light. As Kevin saw him and gave a surly lift of his chin and not a word, Jimmy realised he had to speak.

"I been up at Betty's."

"So what?" Kevin's voice was loud. He was discomforted at seeing Jimmy.

"She called me in to help her with Eva."

"I dunno what you're talkin' about, Jimmy!"

"Oh yeah, you do. You're goin' to finish off what you started. Wassat you got under your arm? A black bin bag?" He had the sickening association of Eva's body in the black bag.

"Lissen," Kevin roared, "you're dumb. You don't know nothin' and for your own health you better keep it that way!"

"You're gonna hurt Betty."

Kevin moved past him to the stairs. "Take notice of what I said, asshole!" he yelled flinging the words over his shoulder.

When Jimmy returned to Number 10 Pew Street the inmates of the shelter were settled for the night and Paul said he didn't need any help. In any case, a bell had been rigged up in Jimmy's room so he could be summoned. Standing in the curry odour of the empty kitchen, he told Paul Emmett what he had seen. Paul listened, not looking directly at him, still and emotionless.

"Tough," Paul said, turning away.

Jimmy went upstairs to his third-floor room with his curry and rice. He'd seen a few corpses before today, but he felt depressed by the waste of a once pretty girl. He ate the now cold food sitting on his bed with the plate on his knees. Then he had a nearly icy shower in the huge bathroom on the floor.

Up to about seventy years ago, the bathroom was used communally by the preachers who stayed overnight at St Edith's; there were four showers, two baths, and two lavatories. The bodily odours of generations of the pious had been absorbed in the grouting around the cracked, yellowed tiles and there was a pervasive and ineradicable smell. Paul Emmett described it as the 'stench of religion'. Now, Jimmy and Paul, who had a room as manager of the shelter, had the whole, otherwise deserted floor to themselves – as well as the bathroom which they shared.

Jimmy had just returned to his room after the shower when he heard Toby Friabin's voice outside.

"You there, Jim-boy?"

"Wassup, Toby?" He opened the door in a t-shirt with a greyish towel around his waist.

"Sorry to disturb your well-earned rest my lad. But I've just asked Paul if I can borrow you, subject of course to your own agreement. A little job, take an hour. Over at the Dog & Duck."

"What is it, Toby?" He spoke cautiously. It was after midnight.

"Tell you when we arrive at that fair hostelry."

Jimmy was usually compliant with Toby. Toby was the voluntary assistant director of St Edith's Settlement which, in addition to the Night Shelter, operated a battered woman's refuge and a drop-in centre for locals in another nearby building.

Jimmy pulled on his clothes and followed Toby out of the rear door of St Edith's, past the shelter where the drifters were now in their bunks, past the dying fire in the yard, across the junk strewn lot, to Butchers' Row. The Dog & Duck was a grimy old public house across the road from the Victorian tenements.

As they chose their path, Jimmy said, "Y' know Eva's been iced, Toby?"

Toby didn't stop, didn't look at him, but went on kicking through the cans. "Eva? Oh, yeah, Eva. Bloody hell! How do you know?"

"Her body was in Ma Thrussell's."

Toby stomped ahead without turning or replying. Jimmy wondered why because Toby usually had a big appetite for gossip, reliable and unreliable.

As they crossed the road to the Dog & Duck, they could see the boozers through the dust on the ground floor windows and hear the thump of rock music. Toby led Jimmy through a side door which he unlocked and up two flights of stairs where rooms were available for hire. He switched on the lights as they entered a dining room with other rooms leading off, now deserted. The stained white-clothed tables were littered with plates containing the remains of food, empty liquor bottles and glasses. Jimmy could tell it had been a swanky show from the champagne flutes and bottles and the scattering of the publican's best silver plate.

Toby was puffing from the exertion and not able to speak for a moment.

"What's goin' on?" Jimmy pressed.

"This is where we're going to clean up in double quick time, my son."

"I don't get it."

"Well, I'll confirm what your eyes are already telling you," Toby said, beginning to gather plates and bottles together. "It's the remains of a party."

"Yeah, yeah. I got eyes, ain't I? Why now? Don't the people who hire the rooms have cleanin' arrangements?"

"We think it ought to be done now. Are you going to help me, Jimmy?" Toby sounded a note of urgency in his voice.

Jimmy was standing with his hands on his hips surveying the mess. "Who's 'we', Toby?"

"Are you going to help, son?"

"Sure, but…" He remained standing still.

Toby halted his noisy clattering of crockery and faced Jimmy. "I'll tell you. Our esteemed board members, or some of them, have had a little knees-up."

Jimmy didn't reply at first; he scowled. "I can smell something, Toby. Does this have anything to do with Eva's death?"

Toby, who had been stacking dishes and removing table cloths, paused again. His plump, usually pasty face was red. His eyes moved around guardedly. "Whaddya mean, lad?" He had a tone of innocent surprise.

"Eva's dead. I told you. Betty Thrussell called me over tonight. The body was in her place. Eva was in party gear like she'd been workin'."

"Terrible," Toby said, concentrating on the dirty plates.

"Don't bullshit me, Toby. You want to clear this place before the cops find it. You already know about Eva."

Toby shook his head fiercely. "Never. No! I got a call from Hassett. He said there had been a problem. That's all he said. A problem. And could I hose the place down with effect from now. He was very insistent. And he pointed out that as organiser of the bunfight I could share in the problem."

"A problem?" Jimmy said derisively.

"Yeah. He told me not to ask questions but to get on with it!"

"Now I'm answering your questions, Toby, an' I dunno a damn thing! It was murder."

"Look, my boy, I don't want to be dragged into anything, but I could be. I put it together. It's a regular thing once a year or so. Food, drink and girls. What's wrong with that?"

"Nothin', unless one of them nobs commits murder."

"Are you going to help me, my son?"

Every instinct of Jimmy's was telling him to go down the stairs and back to his room. But he couldn't do that. He owed Toby. And he thought Toby wasn't just using him. Toby, usually the most composed and confident man in Butchers' Row, was scared too; he needed help. "OK," Jimmy said hesitantly.

He worked silently in a cloud of worry. He filled refuse bags with food scraps, plastic wrappers, cardboard containers and empty bottles. He left the stacked plates and glasses ready for return downstairs to the publican, but Toby insisted that they should be rinsed first.

"They got machines in the kitchen," Jimmy said.

"We have to do the job properly ourselves, Jim-boy."

"Nothin' much you can do about those couches and

cushions and sheets and stuff in the other rooms, Toby. Less you burn 'em."

Jimmy had looked at the other rooms without touching anything. The soiled couches and settees had a turmoil of sheets and rugs over them. He saw pills on the floor, grains of powder on one of the small tables, underneath one chair a hypodermic syringe, an empty condom packet on another chair. He didn't look in the waste baskets; he decided he wouldn't even remove the empty bottles and glasses from those rooms.

"We'll wipe the bottles, the woodwork and take the sheets an' towels," Toby said.

"Don't touch 'em!"

Jimmy appreciated Toby's fatherly interest in him. And he usually respected Toby's advice, but tonight Toby had lost his benign calm. His usual genial expression had set like a papier mâché mask. His eyes had contracted into two gleaming points. Jimmy thought it was a mask of fear. And he was unnerved himself.

Toby continued with the work silently, apparently offended by Jimmy's critical and half-hearted response.

"I ain't touchin' the towels an' sheets an' that or the drugs, Toby."

"OK, boy."

But Toby clearly wanted Jimmy to be there while he finished the task and Jimmy stayed.

2

Little persuasion had been necessary to get Jimmy Morton to forgo his first job as a cleaner at St Edith's Settlement and to learn the craft of begging. Life on the street promised to be much more pleasant than scrubbing floors and lavatories. Jimmy was discovered, as it were, by Toby Friabin. As a local boy, Jimmy already knew Toby by sight; corpulent, tousle-headed and loquacious, a village personality and everybody's friend. They had met when Jimmy cleaned Toby's office at St Edith's. Toby was often in occupation at late hours when the room needed to be cleaned. Lively exchanges of chit-chat followed. And Jimmy was conscious that Toby watched him and goaded him.

On a day when Kate Martin, the director of St Edith's, was also in the room, Toby said, "This lad has charisma, Kate."

Jimmy knew what charisma was, but he'd never thought of himself as having it; bloody cheek was a more apt description.

Kate looked surprised, as though she'd never noticed. "Yes, you're probably right."

"He's not best used sweeping floors."

"He does a good job."

"Of course, but he needs promotion."

"We need the cleaning done."

"There's ten, maybe thirty, good cleaners to one Jimmy."

"What are you suggesting, Toby?"

"The street. The old tin cup. With that smile and line of patter. He's a winner. Guaranteed."

All this was said as though Jimmy wasn't present.

"Do you want to go out collecting for St Edith's, Jimmy?" Kate asked him.

"There's coin in it, lad," Toby added.

"What's the deal?" Jimmy asked. Doing small jobs for years had made him careful.

"Half of what you take is the way we work," Toby said.

Jimmy knew more than one of Toby's collectors and they all declared it was 'a good thing'. He didn't know how much money they actually made because they were inveterate liars.

"Besides, Jimmy's got a supreme asset." Toby swivelled round in his chair, leaning back, legs open, giving full space to his belly.

Kate stopped flicking through a file of papers. Jimmy leaned on his broomstick. Toby slapped his lower leg and widened his eyes significantly.

Kate flinched. "Toby, I'm not sure…"

Jimmy wasn't embarrassed by the reference to his left leg, withered and slightly bent at birth; it wasn't really that bad. And remarks had been made about it ever since he could remember; it was a defect he used to his own advantage at times.

"Come here, lad. Walk up to the door, there and back."

"No, Toby," Kate protested.

But Jimmy chirpily obeyed.

"You can do better than that, Jimmy!" Toby urged.

"Toby, please…" Kate closed her file and rapped her fist on the cover.

"I want a real lurch, Jimmy, plenty of sway. Rock and roll!"

Jimmy obliged with a grin. The curve of the leg was slightly displayed in the tight jeans, indisputably not a gimmick.

"Ah, ha! Yes." Toby was the theatrical director. "When you roll like that, the sympathetic citizen will think, 'There, but for the grace of God or Lady Luck, depending on beliefs, go I.' Don't you agree, Kate?"

"I don't know. I don't want to stand in the way. Find me another cleaner."

"The sight of Jimmy in action will hasten the giving hand to the change-pocket." Toby spoke with conviction.

"He can go on with his night security duties," Kate asserted.

"Certainly. Always remember, Jimmy," Toby said, "the more marked the lurch, the more reliable the donation."

Thus, Jimmy was drafted into the craft of begging and found Toby's aphorism to be true. A few days after this meeting, Toby gave Jimmy an introductory lecture about begging: who to target, what to wear, how to place himself on the street, what to say, and how to deal with the police. Then Toby presented him with a placard inscribed, *St Bernard's, A Charity for Lost Dogs.*

"But I thought I was going to be collecting for St Edith's," Jimmy said.

"A little maybe." Toby moved his large head from side to side as though it was a difficult matter. He pulled out another placard headed, *St Edith's, A Refuge for the Homeless.* "You'll be doing St Edith's sometimes."

"But what's St Bernard's?"

Toby stared calculatingly at Jimmy; then he moved to a cupboard behind his desk which he threw open. "All right, then. You're entitled to know. That is St Bernard's." He pointed to a pile of yellowing papers.

"That's St Bernard's?" The half-inch high thickness of sheets of typescript were curling and dusty and had no meaning for him.

"Yes, it's an about-to-be-registered charity." Toby had a bland expression.

"When?"

"It was about to be registered five years ago, and it's still about to be registered."

"It doesn't look as though it's about to be anythin'. Where are the dogs?"

"Jimmy, my son, *we* are the dogs, and *this* is the dog's home." Toby raised his forefinger and pointed at the roof.

"Gotcha," Jimmy said.

"You see, it's much easier to collect money for dogs, than for people." Toby had a doleful look.

Jimmy nodded vaguely. "I hadn't thought about it."

"And this market cannot be ignored. *Dogs*. A sad comment on the human condition. Hundreds of thousands of dogs in London. All those little shitters going walkies every day. Some run away. Some are abandoned. Kicked out. Hence St Bernard's. But who are we to deny market forces or the soppy side of human nature?"

Toby tightened his mouth at the impossibility of a denial. He held up a placard with a coloured picture of a maimed dog on it. "A shake of the tin, a wide smile with a wobble from you, my boy, will evoke pound coins like four lemons on a slot machine."

Jimmy had found that Toby was right. He became aware that he could collect several times as much money for St Bernard's as he could for St Edith's. Children stopped their parents in the street, pointing at the maimed dog. The parents were honour-bound to show their children that they cared. He had also found that a sweep through the pubs around Piccadilly yielded many a coin from soggy hearts marinated in beer. And old ladies were pushovers.

"We make a token payment to St Edith's of course. We must be transparent and fair."

"What's the St Bernard's money for, Toby?"

Toby wriggled his lips while he thought. "Contingencies," he said finally.

"What contingencies?"

"You know, Jimmy, we all need a smacker at times."

"Sure. But you're collecting more than a smacker."

"True…very true. I will tell you in plain English. It's used, *inter alia*, for… what we call 'insurance'."

Jimmy wasn't sure what *'inter alia'* meant and he let that go. "You mean paying off cops and councillors?"

"My lad, you're wise beyond your years."

"What does Kate say?"

"Nothing," Toby smiled. "She shares my view that charity is good. Even charity for dogs. Therefore, this money is blessed and always available to dogs in need."

"Does that include me?" Jimmy asked.

"You, my son, have joined our team."

Jimmy returned to St Edith's on the Northern line after an afternoon begging in the City around Moorgate. The time was 6pm. It was no use working in the dark. He had a haversack over his shoulder containing his placards and his two full collecting tins. On the Underground he watched critically as two Romanian gypsies, a man with a violin, and a girl singer with a tanned and swelling chest, tried to work between stops; they collected almost nothing in Jimmy's crowded carriage. The passengers, in appearance mostly Asians, Indians, Africans and Chinese were stony in their refusals or mutely embarrassed and looked away. The sad melody of the violin which cried of the ghetto did not ring well in that space, but Jimmy put a pound coin in their collection box. A colleague's salute. The giving gave him a warm spurt; the same feeling he knew his customers savoured as they filled his own tins.

Jimmy had an open, earnest, surprised expression, a ready smile and yet the sallow skin and pinched look of the deprived. He was clean-shaven, with short fair hair. Toby Friabin said he had 'an attractive demeanour for a beggar'. He wore what Toby called a 'uniform': ragged jeans and a denim jacket with holes in the elbows, over a white t-shirt with St Edith's Night Shelter printed across the chest. The garments were well washed, the t-shirt shone. Toby insisted on a clean presentation. Jimmy was a beggar you could almost touch.

He alighted at London Bridge. He walked south of the river from the Underground station and cut through the Southwark Cathedral grounds. The east wind blew up the river. The Thames expelled the cold breath over its banks. He was soon almost alone as he penetrated the maze of damp, ill-lit streets; those around St Edith's were huddled beneath railway viaducts. Winter nights, if they ever went away, returned here at three in the afternoon. Long, chill shadows crept through the brick alleys. A few neon lights choked in steam and smoke. The air was thick with a smell of refuse bins and exhaust fumes, overcome occasionally by a whiff of pizza or fried fish. Although the way was nearly deserted as Jimmy progressed, the vibration of traffic a block or two away and the rumble of trains overhead was ceaseless. He crossed Marshalsea Street and Jarndyce Place and started along Butchers' Row past the ruined tenement where he used to live; it was still partly occupied, with most of the ground floor flats boarded up.

St Edith's Settlement, Jimmy's destination, named after an Anglo-Saxon nun of the tenth century (he had been told), had occupied the same building in Southwark since 1895. Originally it had been a proud red brick structure on four floors, with an elaborate tiled entrance, a chapel, accommodation for priests and lay missionaries and a boy's club. The preachers of the early days arrived on their days-off from other work, or on weekends; they preached the Anglican Christian gospel to the heathen crews of the vessels which then clogged the Thames docks and their families in the nearby slums. Gone, now, as the second millennium had advanced thirteen years, were the vessels and their crews, but what had not changed since 1895 was the pressure of people needing other than religious help. For more than a hundred years, St Edith's had provided from its narrow purse, moving slowly to the edge of bankruptcy.

Jimmy picked his way along the uneven paving of Pew Street, head down. St Edith's was in a desert between the railway arches. What had, a century ago, been a prime site from which to launch the offensive to convert the poor and ignorant, was now in a back alley used by delivery vehicles for factories and warehouses.

Jimmy passed the cracked brickwork of number ten and entered the pillared entrance. This portal had at one time been topped by a stone bust of the founder, Bishop Dunstan. The bishop's head had been broken off and disappeared, leaving only his gowned shoulders and chest. Pieces of the cornice over the door had fallen away. The name 'St Edith's' fashioned in corroded brass letters studded into the wall, had the letter 'E' at a slant on a loose stud.

Jimmy entered and climbed the stairs to Toby Friabin's room. A gloom pervaded the interior halls that was not merely the absence of light outside. The few bare electric bulbs struggled unsuccessfully to illuminate the bile coloured wallpaper and the tobacco-stained ceilings which had not been redecorated in living memory. The reverberations of the Christian message had long since died in these halls with their threadbare carpet strips and faded Victorian prints.

Toby was waiting for the tins with Kate Martin in attendance. Toby's expression, as usual, was good humoured with a calculating edge behind it. He broke the seals and poured the coins on to the table. His thick and dirty fingers flattened the pile and sorted them dexterously into countable fives.

"Four hundred and twenty-three pounds twenty, and two tenner notes. That's an exceptional afternoon's work, my young friend."

Jimmy basked for a moment in the pleasure of his achievement. The phone buzzed. Toby picked it up quickly. He put his palm over the mouthpiece. "It's Hassett. Downstairs." He addressed Kate with a look of distaste.

He had scarcely replaced the phone when the door opened and a thin man in a closely fitting tailor-made suit stepped across the threshold. The tail flap of his jacket rested jauntily across his buttocks. He had a fluff of ginger hair swept back from a face dominated by a pink, pointed nose. In the dowdy room, he shone. Jimmy recognized him as Duncan Hassett, chairman of the board of St Edith's. Hassett had evidently walked quickly past the receptionist in the foyer and run up the stairs.

"Hello. Just looking in to see the wheels turning," he said, with a foxy smile.

Both Kate and Toby looked uncomfortable. Toby's soft bulk was stilled. Kate reached her hand out toward Hassett's gold cuff-linked shirt sleeve. "Let's go to my office, Duncan."

Hassett eyed the spread of coins and notes on the table. "Counting the ill-gotten gains, eh? Should we be doing it? Collecting pennies, I mean."

"Oh well, it all helps," Kate said, leading him toward the door. "By the way, Duncan, this is Jimmy Morton. You remember. I mentioned him to the board..."

Hassett swung around to Jimmy with a smile like a sunrise. "I've been hearing good things about you." He started to proffer his hand, but he withdrew it quickly.

"How did he know me?" Jimmy asked when Hassett had gone, amazed that he was a person known to the chairman.

"Destined for great things, you are," Toby said.

Jimmy was frequently mystified by the codes used by older people and so he didn't press.

3

The bonfire was the eye of the night society.

Jimmy Morton looked out of the bare window of his room on the third floor at the dark space, lit by the fire. The full extent of the waste area and its piles of rubbish was now virtually invisible. At 3 or 4 pm, somebody had rekindled the flames and thrown a bundle of newspapers, an old mattress and some fence posts on the pile. The resulting blaze would be the social centre in the time before supper was served.

St Edith's Night Shelter was a popular refuge for the homeless in this part of London, having bunks for forty men and women. A gradually increasing number of vagrants would soon gather round the fire, telling jokes, drinking, taking drugs and occasionally fighting, or even in the deeper dark, having sex. Some would just stare at the flames.

Often there were too many people seeking beds and Paul Emmett would dismiss the latecomers coldly. Sometimes there were arguments about who was in and who was out. Violence could be near the surface. Some Afghans, Iraqis, Romanians and North Africans could not speak enough English to understand. Another manager might have let people sleep on the floor, but Paul had no anarchic spirit. He was a bureaucrat with forty beds and catering for forty meals. Although, if he calculated that there was any spare food, he would have it doled out to those who had no place before they were sent away.

Jimmy went downstairs to see Paul and found him

moving through the dormitory rooms, inspecting. The cleaners were putting the final touches to their task and placing bedrolls on the bunks. Although it was cold, all the windows were open to reduce the rotten egg smell of the previous nights' occupation and countless nights before that. The walls had absorbed the breath of generations and nothing, short of demolition, would remove the tinge of misery and decay which permeated the air.

Paul wore a thick anorak against the winter chill and calf-height rubber boots. The floors were still damp from scrubbing away mud, vomit and excreta. Jimmy greeted him and eyed the progress critically, as one who had some responsibility for it.

Although Paul was the manager, he had been and continued to look like a priest in his black shirt and trousers. He gave no spiritual consolation; instead, he separated the inmates when their arguments became violent, administered first aid to those who were wounded or overdosed and called the ambulance, or the police if necessary. If a man asked for a prayer, Jimmy noticed that Paul would turned his blade-shaped face away with a sour smile. Calling Paul 'Father' as some inmates did was not persuasive. Jimmy thought that Paul tacitly encouraged these approaches so that he could reject them bitterly.

Paul and Jimmy reached the ground floor satisfied that the dormitories were ready. The trestle tables were set up for the evening meal, which would soon be delivered by another charity and served from big pots and trays in the kitchen. Paul and Jimmy stood in the back doorway, looking across to the figures around the fire, grotesque silhouettes in their layers of t-shirts, jerseys, charity-shop jackets and old overcoats. The fire crackled and sparked. The hoarse conversations were threaded with raucous cries.

Although some of the crowd seemed old in the firelight, Jimmy doubted whether there was a man or woman much over forty-five. The habitual homeless didn't live long. A man who looked sixty might be twenty years younger. The youngest were kids of fifteen or sixteen, some of them runaways who thought it was cool to be on the road. Paul received a monthly list of missing and wanted persons from the police, but it did not receive his close attention.

Jimmy had another official function here. He helped to keep order. Paul could never have managed the whole unruly band on his own. Nor were his volunteer helpers from the suburbs in their warm, neat clothes much use in this. Their pride in their personal virtue brightened their eyes but not their practical skills. The vagrants regarded them with tolerant amusement; an easy touch for a fiver.

To maintain order, Paul used what he described as 'the best prison and boarding school practice'. He knew, because he had been to both. The group policed itself. Two cleaners who were former inmates and Jimmy, with a measure of threatened violence and by capitalising on deference, ruled like prefects in a school or trusties in a prison. Paul reasoned with his enforcers when he thought their decisions unfair, but mostly he let them be. St Edith's Night Shelter fulfilled its purpose – dealing out swift and arbitrary justice for breaches of the peace and providing showers, laundry facilities, a meal and clean dry beds for the homeless with a minimum of fuss. Jimmy's small part was usually accomplished without physical force.

He noticed a boy was standing on a pile of bricks about fifty yards from the fire. He looked cold and too apprehensive to approach. He might have been fifteen. He was wearing a baseball cap and a leather jacket which shone in the firelight. He had a dog with him, a black and white fox terrier. The boy wasn't really noticed; some of those at the fire looked round casually and then returned their attention to the flames.

A few minutes later Jimmy heard shouts and cries. Both he and Paul were tuned in to those desperate kinds of sound.

"Better go see," Paul said to Jimmy.

The boy and a man were down in a pile of wire and tin cans. Jimmy didn't hurry, and before he could get there, the dog attacked the man, throwing itself on to his thighs and buttocks in a fury of gnashing jaws and hysterical barks. The man rolled off the boy, bellowing. This was the kind of play that the fire-watchers appreciated and they switched their gaze to the melee. The man staggered to his feet, hitching up his trousers. He snatched up a short length of iron pipe, swiped at the dog and missed. The boy jumped up and tried to grab the pipe. The man thrust him away and swung at the dog again. This time he connected with the animal's flank; it rolled over yelping. The man raised the pipe for the kill.

Jimmy intercepted the pipe, and jerked it out of the man's hands. "Don't go there, mate," he said quietly.

The man held his arm up to shield himself and after a breath, mumbled, "I won't touch the fuckin dog – 'less somebody stews it for supper!"

He got a laugh from the watchers. "Yeah, let's roast it!" somebody said.

Jimmy bent down beside the dog; it was mewling with pain. "We'll take him inside," he said to the boy.

"Hey, Paul. No dogs inside," a voice said.

It was a well-policed rule that the smelly and often flea and lice ridden dogs of the homeless had to be tied up under the lean-to outside.

Paul hesitated. "It's OK, the animal's sick," he said wearily.

"Well, that means I can take Prince inside!" A man with an overweight retriever appealed to the crowd, but nobody approved him.

Jimmy carried the dog inside. He fetched a box and a hessian sack from the kitchen. He put the box on the floor of the laundry and lined it with the sack. The boy watched silently, hands deep in his jacket pockets. Jimmy laid the dog inside the box.

"I dunno much about dogs," he said to the boy. "Maybe a night's rest will do it. What's y'name?"

"Joe."

"Where from?"

The kid shrugged. "Around."

"Whaddya call the dog?"

"Butch."

"OK, Joe. We'll take a look at Butch in the mornin'. You better see Paul about a bunk."

"Thanks… I know the story. I've been here before."

"Take care, or you'll have somebody in your pants."

Jimmy's stare went slowly down the boy's jacket and jeans to his trainers. He raised his hand, touched the collar of the boy's plaid shirt and let his fingertips rest on the leather jacket. "Sixty quid the shirt, a hundred and fifty the jacket, fifty the jeans, a hundred the Nikes. Nice. *And* a dog, huh?"

"You sure know a lot about threads. You in the rag trade?" the kid asked.

Jimmy just stared at the smooth face; smooth, but slightly hollowed, a glassy tiredness around the eyes. Not a hard face, but hardening.

Joe moved uncomfortably. "Look, thanks for what you

did out there. I mean…"

"Who are ya?" Jimmy grabbed the tag at the boy's chest, unzipped the jacket violently and shoved his hands inside.

"Get off, you bastard!" The boy jumped back as Paul Emmett came in the door.

"What're y' doing to him, Jimmy?"

"Goddam," Jimmy said in his level, seen-it-all voice, "It's not a *him.*"

Jimmy kept watch in the hall between the men's and women's sections for a while after lights-out, as part of his duty. Although many of the inmates had had showers and washed and dried their clothes in the machines which churned in the basement, he still breathed the smell of sweaty underclothes and tobacco. He listened to the rattle of rheumy lungs and the beginnings of the nightmare howls of fevered minds.

After his duty he climbed up to his room, ate his meal, and was lying on his bed fully clothed reading the *Daily Mail* when the rickety door rattled loudly.

"You in there, Jimmy?"

"Yeah." He recognised the phlegmy voice of Bill Sneed, the local Criminal Investigation Division Detective Sergeant. His heart was beating faster. He had expected the call. Sneed, nicknamed 'The Collector', was well known in the area. Jimmy opened the door and instinctively blocked the way.

"Hullo, my friend." Sneed was thin with a yellow face and close-together eyes which pried, past Jimmy, into the room behind him. He wore a baggy grey suit. His green tie had a greasy knot. He opened his lips, on gapped teeth in a grin. "A nice boy like you wouldn't be involved in anything bad. Never."

"What?" Jimmy put the question without expression.

Betty Thrussell had talked – as he expected she would.

"Say sexual assault, say rape, say murder. Whaddya reckon?"

"I don't know nothin'."

"You know what I'm talking about, boy. Somebody has done a filthy thing on our patch and my beloved Chief Inspector has asked me to help clean up."

"Whaddya want from me?"

"I want you to act like a law-abiding citizen – which you are not – and come with me to the station. I'll even let you meet my dear Chief Inspector. What about that?"

Jimmy knew CI Turk by sight and repute, a scowling pillar of a man over six feet tall and seventeen stone, with bunched fists and a reputation for violence.

Jimmy was no stranger to police questioning. He never spoke nor responded to Sneed's jocular remarks in the police car on the way to Jarndyce Street.

"You're not your usual sunny self," Sneed said. "You worried? You should be."

When they were inside the station Sneed led the way down to the basement. All Jimmy's previous experiences had been on the ground floor. He was told to wait in a room which was curiously bare. The floor was flagged and the walls whitewashed concrete. It was chilly and the light was dim. After a few minutes during which Jimmy worried what was going to happen to him, the door opened to admit Chief Inspector Turk in shirtsleeves. His neckless, shaven head disappeared into a white collar held tight by the regulation black tie, his large, jet coloured eyes seemed inhumanly cold. He towered over Jimmy.

"Well, sonny," he said, hooking two fingers into the neck of Jimmy's t-shirt and jerking him forward and backward. "Mr Sneed tells me you're ready to confess." He rocked

Jimmy until there was a tearing sound from his t-shirt.

"I got nothin' to confess." Jimmy kept his arms at his sides and took the shaking; it was an unwritten rule. Shut up and submit. He'd liked to have kicked this gorilla in the balls, but that was the way to a shed-load of charges and prison.

"Everybody's got something to confess, Morton, and a little turdface like you more than most!" He placed the palms of both hands flat on Jimmy's chest and gave him a violent push.

Jimmy staggered back and hit the wall. Turk was up against him, pressing his shoulders back against the concrete. He slapped Jimmy's face, left cheek, then the right, hard enough to hurt but not to bruise.

"I'm going to get you ready for your confession by giving you a decent kicking around this room, Morton." Pleasure sparked in Turk's expression. "Scared?"

Turk was said to be a specialist in decent kickings. Jimmy understood the bare room now. No furniture to get in the way. No cameras or tapes.

"I got nothin' to confess."

"Think of something, laddie." Turk gripped his shoulders and shook him, irritated at the lack of response. "You're a little dummy, aren't you? No guts." Turk spun him around and kicked him in the arse. He rammed Jimmy chest-forward into the wall, taking care to see that Jimmy took the impact on his chest.

"This is just a warm-up, sonny. Soon you'll be fuckin' singing!" He slapped Jimmy again across the left ear, then the right.

Jimmy's head was reeling. The door opened and Sneed, file in hand, sidled in. He stopped on the threshold, looking but not seeing.

"Just getting your boy sorted out," Turk joked. "He tells

me he's got a lot to tell you. Get on with it. I'll be waiting."

Sneed, dead-eyed, watched Turk go out of the door. He jerked his head to get Jimmy to follow him to an interview room along the corridor. Jimmy sat down stinging and burning but bearing no marks that would support a complaint. He'd had this treatment before from other cops. He sighted the camera in the ceiling of the interview room. He was probably safe enough here.

Sneed fiddled with the recorder. "OK, ready. Now, your name is James Morton, you reside at St Edith's Settlement, and you're a cleaner..."

"Charity collector and supervisor at the Night Shelter."

Sneed switched the recorder off. "You're also a lying little maggot!"

He switched the recorder on. "I'm interviewing you in connection with the rape and murder of Magdalena Walecka, known as Eva Walecka at Butchers' Row, Southwark..." He switched the recorder off.

"Tell me why you did it, Jimmy?"

The monstrosity of the allegation was frightening even though it was nonsense. "I didn't do nothin' to nobody."

"Where were you last night?"

"My head's sore. Mr Turk banged me about."

Sneed reached for the recorder switch. "Don't come that one!"

Jimmy had learned to try to get his story on the record, because although Sneed would not hesitate to edit and delete from the tape, it made work more difficult for him. When Sneed threateningly turned the recorder on again, Jimmy said, "Mr Turk said to you ..." Sneed switched off. "He said to you that he'd been sorting me out when you came to get me. He slapped me round. I've got a headache."

"Don't moan to me you little slimeball. Let's get on with it. Your whereabouts?" Sneed switched on the recorder.

"I got back to the St Edith's Settlement building in Pew Street about 4pm. I was working there at about 10pm or 11pm when Betty Thrussell came over. She said something terrible had happened and would I go to her place."

"She lives at Butchers' Row a few hundred yards away. And you know her, right?"

"Right. She used to be my landlady. She wouldn't tell me what it was about."

"Why did you go, then?"

"Because she's a friend, and she was, y' know, upset."

"You're a gentleman. What did you find?"

"Eva was in the hall on the floor."

"Of Ma Thrussell's flat? You know Eva?"

"I've spoken to her, just a few words."

"Where?"

"In Harry's Coffee shop."

Sneed switched off. "You've fucked her, haven't you?"

"Never been near her."

Sneed switched on. "Why speak to her in the coffee shop? Boy fancies girl, eh?"

"Nah. I wouldn't touch her. She's owned by a guy."

"Why speak to her, then?"

"I dunno. She was a face in the Row and around."

"What did you do when you saw the body?"

"Nothin'. I told Betty to call the cops."

"Why didn't you?"

"None of my business. Shit, it was in her home!"

"Come on, Jimmy. You were in the flat earlier."

"No, I told you."

"What else did you tell Betty Thrussell?"

"Not to shift the body." He realized too late that he didn't need to say this.

"Why should she want to?"

"Because it was in her place."

"No. It was to keep her son Kevin out of the picture, wasn't it?"

"I dunno."

"You know Kevin. He's a mate of yours."

"Not a mate of mine."

"You know Eva's pimp?"

"I've seen him around."

"How'd you know he was her pimp?"

"Because everybody knows what's goin' on in the Row."

"So, you just walked out of Butchers' Row after five minutes of advising?"

"Yeah."

"Then why does Ma Thrussell say she doesn't know anything about anything except the body being found in the corridor *outside* her place and she called you in?"

"That's what she said? She's lyin'. The body was in her hall. I sure as hell never moved it. Betty is a friend of mine. I wouldn't do anythin' to hurt her. But that's the truth."

Sneed switched the recorder off.

"Oh, just a point. You touched the body when you were looking at it?"

"I told you. No way. "Whyn't you recordin' what I say?"

Sneed gave a nasty grin. "I think we'll find your DNA on the body."

"No way. Howya know my DNA?"

"You're a regular cleverdick, aren't you?" Sneed leaned back in his chair and picked his nose. "This is very unsatisfactory. I think you're telling porky pies. CI Turk is going to be very displeased. He will want to continue his chat with you on another day himself. Get out of here!"

Jimmy stumbled and half-ran back through the freezing streets to St Edith's but the worst chill was inside him.

4

The girl occupied a bunk in the small room usually reserved for women. The men and women may have glanced at her curiously at times while eating and getting to their bunks, but the interest was short-lived; a glance at an unusual moth. They were more focused on what was smouldering inside their heads; the image of the next needle, the next slug of whisky, the next spliff, the next tot of methadone, the next snort of coke. Although sexual predation and drunken violence could flicker or even explode at times amongst the inmates, their interest in each other was detached and transitory, like passengers on a bus who intend to get off at the next stop. But that didn't prevent a lot of elbowing and shoving and shouting and abuse; it didn't stem the undercurrent of turbulence, which suggested that violence was near.

One of Jimmy's morning duties, with his fellow trusties, was to clear out the sleepers. He found the girl huddled under a blanket. He ignored the grumbling from the women at his intrusion; some were not yet dressed, although most slept in their street clothes. He shook the girl. She poked a startled, wide-awake face at him. He was interested in her, but he knew that people who used the shelter each towed a story behind them like a creaking, overloaded cart. He couldn't work out whether the girl was a delicate flower who would wilt in this environment or a savvy operator.

"Let's get somethin' to eat and maybe get the hell outta here," he said.

The inmates were mostly out of bed, moving around unsteadily like sleepwalkers; some sat on their bunks and stared into space, grunting, burping, farting, preparing to face the cold of the day. The girl's presence or absence was as irrelevant to them as theirs was to each other. Jimmy went with her to look at the dog. It was sitting up in its box making low crying noises.

"Looks OK to me," he said, going away and returning with a bone from the refrigerator.

The girl went to the washroom where she could splash water on her face, dry off with a paper towel and use one of the shelter's disposable toothbrushes. Breakfast was a big mug of milky coffee and a rough-cut chunk of toasted bread, with a fried egg on top. The smell of frying eggs overcame the reek of the night.

"What're you goin' to do?" Jimmy asked, not looking at her as they chomped the toast.

"I dunno."

"You wanta stick around?"

"Can I?" It was a plea.

"You wanta work, right?"

"What sort of work?" She had an aloof tone.

"I'll show you."

"What if I'm no good?" Very throwaway.

She was playing tough but he didn't think she was tough. He thought she formed her words to make them sound rough, when they would have been pronounced more like the way Kate Martin spoke.

"You don't know nothin', right? I said I'd show you."

He rose to his feet and snapped his fingers. "Gimme the jacket and shoes."

She looked miserable. She peeled off the jacket and kicked off the trainers. "Why? I'm cold."

Her shirt sleeves were rolled up. She began to roll them down, but not before he saw the marks on her forearm. He grasped her arm and looked more closely.

"Lemme go!"

He saw a line of small, red blotches some of which were scabby sores on the white almost hairless flesh. She looked at him angrily, pulling her arm away. He released her and scooped the clothes up leaving her at the table, shivering. When he came back she was watching as the man opposite to her, the only other person at the table, smeared egg yolk over his beard. He was pushing lumps of bread past his broken teeth with his fingers. The man swung his rheumy eyes toward her. "Wassa fuck's the matter?" His voice grated; he spat out dobs of the bread.

She looked away; she saw Jimmy was holding a torn cotton shirt, a navy blue wool sweater, a rundown pair of blue training shoes and a baseball cap.

"Put these on. Better change your shirt too. Go inside to get it off and give it to me."

"Where are my clothes?" she asked weakly.

"Don't worry. I have 'em."

"Why do I have to change?"

"Because you can't do our thing lookin' as though you just stepped outta the Ladies' Department at Harvey Nichols."

The girl changed her shirt, put on the jersey and shoes and pulled the Yankees' baseball cap down over her face. Jimmy inspected her critically.

"Pull your hair out from the cap. What happened to y'hair? Somebody slash it?" Her dark hair had been roughly hacked short. "Maybe ditch the cap." He was irritated. "You gotta look like a girl. Stick y'chest out, will ya?"

At last he was satisfied. His own canvas shoes were worn.

His jeans were rubbed white in places. His old anorak was frayed at the cuffs. But he looked clean.

"Right. Now get the dog. He's part of the act. Put this round his neck and keep him near you." He gave her a frayed piece of sash cord.

"There's a leather lead in the pocket of my jacket."

"Just what you don't need."

She looked uneasy. Her wary glance suggested that they were disguising themselves to do something disreputable. When Jimmy led her on to the street, he had two cards about twelve inches square under his arm. She couldn't see the writing on them because they were together face-to-face. And he had a haversack over one shoulder. They walked up by London Bridge, into the City. She began to get tired and the shoes hurt her feet. Jimmy took no notice of her, moving quickly despite his slight limp. Butch trotted on the rope, recovered and unconcerned.

After a while he asked, "What's y' name?"

"Josie."

He didn't speak otherwise. When they arrived at Lombard Street, an area of banks and insurance companies, Jimmy stopped at the entrance to a church near Sherborne Lane. He mounted the steps leading to the closed doors, observing the street both ways. It was flowing with a tide of purposefully moving businessmen and women and a few messengers and porters tending delivery vans.

"This is a good beat. We'll work around here till we wear out the crowd or die of exposure."

He drew Josie to a space beside the doors of the church and set down the haversack. He removed a yellow plastic collection box from the pack, with the label 'St Bernard's Dogs Home'. From his pocket, he took a few coins and dropped them into the coin-slot.

"Seedin' the crop," he said, with a momentary grin, as he shook the coins inside to make a noise.

"I get it," Josie said. "All flim-flam."

"Right on." He hung one of the cards by its cord around his neck. Josie was faced with a graphic enlarged photograph in stark black-and-white, showing an injured dog with the caption, 'Give him a home'.

Jimmy surveyed the passers-by carefully. He stepped down to the pavement into the path of a man of about thirty, wrapped in a long navy-blue woollen overcoat. He made sure he caught the man's attention from a few yards away with a movement of his arm and lurched toward him. Jimmy spoke out of earshot of Josie but she watched. The man hesitated, fished in his pocket and produced something which he put in the tin. Jimmy smiled and touched his forehead respectfully. Sure that his performance had been observed by an approaching woman swathed in a long astrakhan coat, he turned to her. She halted, opened her purse and tried to stuff a note in the coin-slot. Jimmy helped her and graciously backed away, returning to the church steps.

"See how it works? A few quid in a few moments. It beats the minimum wage."

"I'm not sure I could do that."

"Your turn. Rattle the box and smile," Jimmy said, placing the other, similar card around her neck.

He mounted a step above her and surveyed those who were approaching. "Now there's a guy, you see… with the stick." He nodded toward a man in a neat blue raincoat, slightly older than the previous target.

"I think a woman would be better…"

"You're already an expert?"

For Jimmy, it was like pushing her off a high diving

board over an icy pool. She owed him. She had to do it.

"This woman," she said. "The one following that bike-messenger. Nice fur collar. Money in her purse, wouldn't you say?"

"Go for it."

She handed him Butch's lead.

"Take the fuckin dog! That's what it's for."

Josie took a deep breath and stepped off, towing Butch. She swayed in front of the woman and said, "Excuse me." It looked for a second as though the woman would walk on; instead, she turned, tangled in the dog's lead. But her fingers went into her purse and produced a note. Josie returned to Jimmy, proud of her efforts.

From then on they took it in turns, choosing their quarry. Most approaches were successful in eliciting at least a few coins, but there was also a supply of ten and five pound notes.

After an hour, Jimmy accosted a youngish man wearing a tan overcoat with dark green velvet lapels. His face was round and red, his thin and greasy black hair swept back over his skull.

"Pound for the dog, guvner?" he said jovially, proffering the tin and obstructing the man's course. He realised too late that he had made a mistake. He was looking at a face that was metallic and mean.

The man swung his arm out, knocking the tin away. "Get away, scum!"

"No need to be violent, shithead!"

"What did you call me?" the man shouted, his mouth opening wide on big teeth as he spoke. He grabbed Jimmy's anorak by the open throat. "We can't walk the streets without being obstructed and insulted by vermin like you!"

Jimmy broke the man's hold with one arm easily. He

backed away defensively. "Get off to your office, you cunt, and get on with fleecing old women!" His tone was even, derisory, a version of a recording played many times.

The people who had crowded past them on the footpath were intent on their own affairs and his assailant was now yards away. The man stalked off, pulling a mobile phone from his pocket meaningfully and gesturing with it towards Jimmy.

Jimmy retreated to the steps, faintly amused. "Gotta choose the mark more carefully," he said to Josie. "And we better move soon or the cops'll be around."

He chose another pitch three blocks away in Cheapside. Hours later when the tins were getting full and heavy, he called a halt. "Let's go get a coffee and a donut."

He found an eatery in an alley off Clement's Lane that seemed to cater for people dressed like them. He tied Butch to the free newspaper dispenser outside. Instead of a donut, he relented to order steak and french-fries for them both. He never asked Josie what she wanted and he checked the prices carefully with the impatient waitress, refusing any side orders.

Josie was like a dog wanting to be stroked. She obviously felt that she had put on a good performance and he ought to be pleased, but he showed no appreciation. The food arrived quickly, slapped down in front of them. They were hungry and absorbed in eating for a while.

"I think it's such a great thing, collecting for a dog's home," Josie said. "Have you ever visited St Bernards?"

His small start was momentary. "Sure."

"What's it like?"

"Pretty awful."

"All those lost and maimed dogs. Sad."

"Better tell me," he said. The tone of his voice was firmer.

"What?" she replied.

"You know what. What's with you?"

Josie reared up in a 'You've got a cheek' gesture. She hesitated but she had to speak. "I was living with a girlfriend. She was using. She swiped my money and disappeared…"

"Howd' you know about St Edith's?"

She paused again. "Somebody told me. I can't remember who."

"You said you'd been before."

"I was trying to… be clever."

"Why'd you move out of where you were living with your girlfriend?"

"I was afraid of her bloke. He was hanging around."

"You were using."

"Not now. I've had a detox."

"Where?"

Another hesitation. "Someplace a community worker dumped me when I was found on the street."

Jimmy weighed this up, forking some shrivelled french fries around in the grease on his plate and trying to work out how fresh the scars on her arm were.

"Where'd you get that jacket you were wearing?"

She crushed her hands together, looking at them; they were white and the nails, trimmed. "A drunk dropped his wallet. My share. A couple of hundred. Bought the jacket. And the other stuff."

Jimmy was thoughtful. Her expression was blasé, saying, 'What do you think of this story? Will it fit or do I have to give you another?'.

"Where you headin'?"

"Get a job, I guess."

"But you can't do nothin'."

"You're right, Jimmy. I can't do anything."

He didn't think she was correcting him. She was a bit worn down and letting herself go. The street had taught him about class and about real and fake, about what was gold and what was gilt. He couldn't tell the distinctions with any certainty. He knew that most likely what he would be offered was fake. It didn't bother him; it just made him more careful. She was a junkie no doubt, but not a low-lifer like she was pretending. The cute dog, the leather jacket, the manicured hands, these were all a zillion miles from his kind of life. But he kept his thoughts to himself.

"You still want in on the job?"

"Oh, yes, please Jimmy," she pleaded the words again.

He received them with an old-man expression. Even though his sallow skin was unlined and his fair hair thick, he seemed to be looking through her to infinity as if he knew every step of the way.

"Thanks." She reached affectionately across the table to place her fingertips on the back of his hand. And then she withdrew realising her gesture was not appropriate. "Where will I stay?"

"I'll see Paul. You can stay at the shelter for a night or so. It's not a free B&B. I can fix you somethin' over the road. Then, we'll see." He had a faded smile as he looked towards the steamy window with the flaking word 'Restaurant' reading backwards on it.

5

Jimmy was troubled by his visit to clean up at the Dog & Duck with Toby Friabin. Sneed's call and Turk's treatment were alarming; he'd experienced 'official' violence before, but not with a murder charge in the air. It wasn't a matter of being innocent and therefore entirely confident. He knew the system didn't work like that. The cops were looking for somebody to hang Eva's murder on; it was scary to think it could be him. He usually enjoyed his days, but now poor Eva cast a cloud over them. He seized the opportunity to talk to Toby on a day when Jimmy had returned the tins and found him alone.

The important man had recovered his poise and ebullience. He was spread-eagled in, rather than sitting on his chair, eating a cream cake. Toby was as wide as a door. His appetite was enormous. He could not resist food, any food, and especially he loved the pies, pasties and sausage rolls, served in Harry's Café, the fragrant little pastry-cookery around the corner from Number 10. At least once a day Toby could be seen in Harry's, munching with glazed eyes.

Toby was a donor to local causes and something of a public figure as the voluntary part-time assistant director of St Edith's and a member of the board of management. He was also a man between in the Butchers' Row community; not by any means poor or disadvantaged, and not precisely a criminal or known to be a member of any local mafia. He owned a used car sale-yard and conducted auctions. He was said to be embroiled in dodgy property deals. It was rumoured that he was involved with hot money from heists and boosted cars, but he had never been charged. Detective Sergeant Sneed was on cordial terms with him.

Toby lived in what Jimmy regarded as considerable splendour in a 'penthouse' apartment. It was actually the top floor of an old building, owned by Toby. He rented the lower floors as a furniture storehouse. The penthouse was half a mile from Number 10, on the fringe of a rundown council housing estate. Jimmy had visited the apartment in his capacity as a porter of bags and parcels and been shown around by a proud Toby. He had no experience of luxurious or tasteful decoration and was suitably impressed by the shag pile carpets, tall mirrors, glass chandeliers, imitation tiger and zebra rugs, garish and thickly daubed oil paintings and the riot of clashing colour in the bulging curtains and sofas. He also noticed the steel entrance door and the razor wire on the fire escape to deter ambitious burglars. In this palace, Toby's plump wife, Amethyst, with skin like snow and yellow curls, was pampered like a poodle. They had no children.

Toby had resolutely stonewalled on the subject of Eva when they were clearing up at the public house and Jimmy had had an increasing feeling of resentment. He was going to demand the opportunity to speak. He sat down in a chair opposite Toby's desk and stared at him.

"My son?" Toby responded, wiping his mouth with the back of his hand and brushing the crumbs off his desk. "I do not see your usually joyful face."

"What happened, Toby?"

"Whaddya mean, my dear boy?" He tried an easy beam, but it became stiff and uneasy.

"Eva."

"No idea." Toby's eyes opened wide and his chubby face emptied of expression.

"You owe me an explanation. You involved me."

"Too true, dear boy, but wouldn't it be better to remain in ignorance?"

"The cops have already been at me. They'll start askin' questions about the Dog and then they'll ask you..."

"I've already been questioned by my dear friend, William Sneed, a lovely man."

"What did you tell him?"

"Nothing. Bill knows I wouldn't, couldn't be involved. Why mention the Dog when the corpus delicti is at Butchers' Row?"

"Oh, yeah? He'll get to you."

"Let's agree that your night at the D&D didn't happen." Toby lifted his shoulders carelessly.

"How can I? I've left prints all over those rooms." Jimmy's voice was now plainly dismissive: "And so have *you*."

Toby paused for thought. "Let's agree that we helped with the banquet earlier in the evening. But earlier, not later, in the remote and unlikely event that Her Majesty's Constabulary ask questions."

"They ain't stupid, Toby. They'll find out there was a party at the Dog if they don't know now. They'll trace Eva's movements on the night. They'll talk to everybody present. Then we could be in deep turd."

Toby appeared to weigh this but was silent.

"What about the bedrooms? All them blankets an' sheets'll have DNA all over'em."

"Ah, the couches. Jim-lad, you have the makings of a forensic scientist."

"Look, Toby, the best story is we cleaned the whole

show up after it was over, at midnight, by arrangement with your guests."

"The truth?" Toby considered this for a time as though it was novel and a last resort. "A sage observation my young friend. Let it be so."

"What about Eva? Did she go to the party?"

Toby nodded warily. "She was there."

"I thought so. Her clothes were a giveaway. I'll never understand why guys like them... do this, Toby."

"I would have thought a fellow of your perspicacity and worldly knowledge would know instinctively. When you have everything, my boy, you want *more and different.* The gentlemen like a bit of rough, don't they? They get bored with champagne and truffles. Fish and chips is what they desire occasionally. Entirely harmless. Private and discreet."

"And the lap-dancing and whoring?"

"Avant-garde cabaret I would have called it. But yes. It's more fun than reading about somebody else doing it in the *Sun* and they can afford it."

"Somethin' musta happened at the party or Hassett wouldn't have got on to you to clean up."

"I think we should forget the honourable gentleman's call to me and take a practical view. I'm thinking here of evidence, clear evidence. Mother Thrussell, you say is or was custodian of the corpse, a matron of reasonable repute for this area, but Kevin her progeny is a right animal. I detect his hand, perhaps his penis. Why would the sleeping princess be in the Ma Thrussell's castle unless young Prince Kevin placed her there?"

"Naah. Somethin' happened at the party an' Kevin was wheeled in to get rid of the body." He spoke emphatically. He knew nothing. His guts were doing the thinking.

"Kevin's a scumbag with plenty of available pussy. Not a sex killer."

Toby splayed his fingers out. "Pure speculation, Jim-boy. And I can't tell you what happened at the party. I wasn't there. It's as much a mystery to me as it is to you."

Jimmy took a long look at Toby's woebegone face and didn't quite believe him.

"I've spoken to Catesby the master of the directors and Hassett," Toby said.

"Why? Why not let the police get around to it?" Again, Jimmy raised his voice.

"Take it easy, my young friend. Because we need to check we are holding the same hymn sheets. Catesby & Co. come here when they could well afford the delights of Soho or King's Cross. Why? Because they don't want to find themselves on the front page of the tabloids. They provide a cheque with no questions asked about costs in return for privacy and discretion. It's a solemn bond which we must honour."

"Provided you don't get involved in their dirty work."

"But yes. I do not intend to go to the scaffold for Arnold Catesby, be he the Lord High Admiral."

"That lot'll be nervous."

"That makes me less nervous," Toby asserted. "Fair sharing. Indeed, they will quake, because even assuming they are all entirely innocent of any wrongdoing, as very important people always are, some little nark in the police force is likely to leak their story to one of our discerning newspapers."

"You're makin' me cry, Toby. And weren't you there?"

"Not me. At least not in the capacity of a guest. I was there to assure myself that food and service were poised, greet the good gentlemen, introduce the girls, have a complimentary beer and vamoose very early in the proceedings."

"And we were there to clean up afterwards."

"We were and not a sign of trouble. I'll have to have a word with the other little ladies who were there…"

"Do I know them?"

Toby looked reluctant to reveal the names, but eventually said, "OK, you're involved. I tell you. You work out your own destiny."

"That's the way I want it."

"One charmer was Madame Thrussell's delightful daughter."

"Gloria? I didn't know she was on the game."

"Jimmy, nothing so crude. She's an escort."

"I dunno the difference."

He had taken Gloria to the movies in the distant past. She was a busty blonde who liked a full English breakfast too much. She had a loud voice and could look after herself. She had trusted Jimmy and there were times, years ago, when he thought he was in love with her. Gloria didn't like stacking shelves at the supermarket. Her ambition had been to have a baby and get married. She didn't think of marriage as a prior step to having a baby. In her mind, the sequence as she explained it, and Jimmy understood it, was to have a baby, set up house on the Benefit and if the bloke liked it enough he'd move in and maybe marry her later; if he didn't, he'd maybe call round occasionally. When or if he stopped coming, she'd be free to get a new bloke. Gloria had moved part of the way toward achieving her ambition. She had produced twins and had been allocated a small council house. She had told Jimmy that she could get a bigger house with every additional child.

"Who else was there?" Jimmy asked.

"Garnet Peabody."

"From the office? That's a bit close to home. What's her specialty?"

"Pole dancing. This was to be an evening of harmless pursuits by civilized gentlemen, dear boy, a little lap-dancing, a tasteful strip-dance."

Jimmy rejected Toby's words with a shake of the head. "I've already been hauled in by Sneed, Toby."

"Betty Thrussell?"

"Yeah. She told him I'd been in the building. She said she called me in when she found the body *in the hall*, where it was found by the cops. She's tryin' to cover for Kevin… and kinda swingin' the nasty my way."

"When a good woman like Dame Thrussell is shielding her only son and dearest child, we can't expect veracity."

"Turk belted me around. The cops don't know nothin' and nor did I. But when they find we cleaned up, we'll get the acid."

Toby stiffened, looked apprehensive, then his shoulders sagged down softly. "Have faith in Uncle Toby, my dearest boy." He slipped a cardboard box out of his desk drawer containing two large and elaborate cream cakes sprinkled with hundreds and thousands. He offered one to Jimmy.

6

Jimmy had been puzzled by Duncan Hassett's remark that Kate Martin had mentioned his name to the board and the reason was swiftly resolved. Hassett was one of that breed of sleekly suited men who appeared to determine how things will be, far beyond Jimmy's compass; and Jimmy, therefore, had some concern when Kate asked him to come to her office. Usually, all his business with Kate could be done as they passed on the stairs. But Kate seemed in good spirits when he presented himself. She offered him a chair and a cup of coffee from the pot on her desk.

Kate was a big woman whose heavy, voluminous dresses made her look pyramidal. She was always very much covered up, from her throat, nearly to her ankles. Her ankles were thick, with heavy walking shoes. She wore her brown hair down to her shoulders, and that too was brushed over her forehead and part of her cheeks. All that was visible of her face was a small expanse of smooth, creamy skin, around a small nose and a pair of clear grey eyes which blinked very slowly. She had a Home Counties accent and she was thirty-five to forty.

Kate was well-liked by the staff. Jimmy knew her as a tough, combative woman, not easily intimidated. She was said to be treated coldly by the board.

"Jimmy, I want to ask you to think about something. You know about the board, don't you?"

"Sure." Jimmy knew. Everybody knew. The ultimate

decision on anything big and on some things very small at St Edith's was, 'The board said…'.

"You've met old Mervyn Kay at the Drop-In Centre, haven't you? He's a local representative on the board like Toby."

"Sure. Merv's lookin' a bit frail."

"I'd like you to take his place. He's getting too old to come to meetings and when he does come he falls asleep."

"Why me? I don't understand."

Sudden elevation to the board of St Edith's seemed like a journey into space and equally mysterious. It was a place he never had the slightest thought that he might go.

"We usually get a regular, like Mervyn, from the Drop-In Centre, to accept an appointment, but there isn't anybody else I could recommend to the board at the moment."

"But I don't know nothin'."

"You don't have to know nothing-anything. Actually, I think you know a lot. I'll go through the papers with you before the meeting. I'll tell you what I want. All you have to do is to support me. You see, my problem is this: there are places for five Ravens and five locals on the board. You know the Ravens, as we call them, are ex-Ravensthorpe public school."

"Sure, I've heard of it."

"St Edith's was set up in the dark ages by Bishop Dunstan. He was also the principal of Ravensthorpe and the school regard St Edith's as 'theirs', with fifty percent of the places reserved for them. With the help of the chairman and the locals and the odd loose cannon on the Raven's side, I can usually swing most of the things I want. If the number of locals falls, the Ravens are likely to get their way."

"What's so bad about the Ravens getting their way?"

"That's something you'll find out about when you join

the board. The fact is we're broke. We've always been broke. We have a couple of buildings in need of repair and the Council is thinking of closing us down. There's a big scheme to build a giant skyscraper on the land around here."

"Yeah. I heard about the skyscraper, must be years ago. One of them things people talk about that never happens. Like Heathrow airport."

"So what do you think?" Kate, palms clasped around her coffee cup, gave him a most engaging and earnest look.

"OK," Jimmy said, slowly. "That's news about being broke and closing. But why *me*, I mean lots of people would like to support you, Kate."

"You'd be surprised how difficult it is to get somebody who's fit and prepared to give up the time to come to meetings…"

"The time's not a problem, but…."

"Don't put yourself down. I have given the board a good story about you. A disabled youth. You're twenty-one. An orphan, honest, industrious and intelligent. You've worked as a volunteer around St Edith's for a few years. Now one of our paid helpers."

"I was a cleaner." Jimmy's face showed cheerful surprise.

"General assistant, now a fundraiser…"

"Beggar!" he laughed.

"Fundraiser. No such thing as a beggar at St Edith's. All right, you've had little schooling. But Paul tells me you read books. You'll understand the business at board level. You can add up. It's all about money. Everything is about money. You know that."

"No kidding I know it."

"You'll understand what's going on, but perhaps not the accounting finesse or legal aspects. But that doesn't matter."

The description only seemed to touch Jimmy at odd

points. He gave his pale smile. "Cut the bullshit, Kate. I'm a homeless school drop-out with a crippled leg who does odd jobs."

Kate shook her voluminous hair in disagreement. "Everything I said about you is true. The Ravens were delighted to hear this, because they consider themselves masters of accounting and legal matters. They'll expect you to be like most of the other local representatives in their eyes, pliable, inarticulate and somewhat stupid."

"Sounds like me." Jimmy gave a small head movement of acceptance. "Does that description include Toby?"

"No. Toby's a one-off."

"Don't you want somebody like… Paul?"

"The Ravens don't want anybody on the other side who is too smart. You can leave the thinking to me."

"Toby's smart."

"He is and he occasionally upsets the board."

"Do *you* want anybody who knows anything, Kate?"

She grinned. "No, not particularly. I just want your vote, Jimmy. You tick all the boxes, as the saying goes. You're young, you're disabled, you're poor and disadvantaged. You could only improve your credentials by also being black and female. I predict you'll be elected unanimously when I put your name forward."

"Why not Paul?"

"Paul's known by the board to be gay."

"Nobody that way on the board?"

"I wouldn't be surprised but not as far as the world's concerned. Look, this will be good experience for you. You can't work the Night Shelter and the street forever."

"OK, then." He spoke uncertainly. He didn't know whether he was doing Kate a favour, or whether he should thank her for doing him a favour.

Kate put her cup down deliberately on the desk and stared at it for a moment, grimacing. "I suppose it's only fair that I tell you what it's like in there," she said, pointing to the wall. The boardroom was next door. For the first time her expression showed a negative feeling, revulsion. She wrinkled her nose. "It's not nice. But you'll get on fine. It's what you know. A maelstrom of dislike and disaffection."

"What's that?"

"The Ravens have prejudices about each other which go back to their schooldays. Most are very successful in their own line of business; the law, banking, stockbroking, antiques, but not enough to stop them envying the estate, or the yacht, or the business coup of the other. They don't like me or the locals much either."

"Why do they bother with St Edith's then?"

Kate paused. "I suppose they think they can cleanse their souls by spending a few hours a month down here and then go back to their villas and yachts. Volunteers have been doing it since 1895."

"They're hypocrites but we're not?"

"Of course we are Jimmy, but when you're poor and have no power, the effect of your hypocrisy is somewhat less. The Ravens have a lot of power and influence and money."

Jimmy didn't know any people with money, apart from Toby Friabin, but in other respects it sounded like what he knew: bitching, envy, lies, dog-eat-dog.

Kate went on surprising him, a beggar, with her candour: "The thread which *unites* the Ravens is a mild and unspoken repugnance for the other half of the board, which will include you. The locals on the board are seen by the Ravens as an ignorant lot who have dirty fingernails and can't spell."

Jimmy looked at his fingernails and held up his hand. "And I can't spell."

"So you'll join me..."

"What about them?" Jimmy countered. "Arrivin' in their big motors. What do they know about Butchers' Row?"

"Ah, yes. A very good point. Well, the Ravens know *everything* because they are clever and well-educated. When they say, *it is so*, it is so. You'll be joining the locals who secretly feel that they alone truly understand the noise and stink and poverty of Pew Street and its environs because they – like you – live here. That's the difference."

"That's OK, then," Jimmy said, unaccountably feeling more satisfied. "What's the pay?"

"None. Nobody gets any. Disappointed?"

"Yeah. How'm I gonna buy a Bentley like them Ravens?"

Jimmy was hesitant and docile at his first meeting with board members and was shortly elected. In action, he confirmed Kate's prediction. She had secured her ally. He appeared to her to be the ideal local representative. He rarely spoke unless addressed, but he did read the papers and try to understand them before meetings with Kate's help. He loyally supported every proposition which Kate put forward.

He soon became used to the tension of the board meetings which were, to him, much less edgy than those around the Night Shelter, where they could erupt in murderous knife-fights. The surging feelings of the Ravens, chafing on each other and the local members, were mostly contained by the chairmanship of Duncan Hassett; they were often evidenced in a curt inflexion of voice, a sigh, or seen in a curling lip, or a head hung in speechless silence. But Kate was right. The meetings took place in twisting currents of disaffection. The locals were a sad and dilapidated little group pushed into a corner by the enormous egos of the Ravens.

Jimmy was bored at meetings and often never listened attentively. It was a relief from the gloom to take the time to admire the shirts and silk ties of the Ravens and their hair, often scanty, but always shampooed and impeccably barbered.

With a staff of twenty, St Edith's was a real presence in the area. Number 10 Pew Street provided the offices and the Night Shelter; and the other decrepit building, in an equally unpromising nearby street, contained the Drop-in Centre for people to have a cup of tea and a game of cards, the counselling service and a refuge for battered women. St Edith's was a costly undertaking.

Obtaining the money to keep these disparate services operating and maintain the buildings was the bane of the board's life, although the collective wealth of the Ravens would probably have sufficed to finance St Edith's for decades. The Ravens seldom made donations but agonized at the meanness of government. The charity relied on funds from local government grants and private donations. St Edith's was also a beneficiary under the wills of a few dead Ravens and heir to several more, but the great hulk that was St Edith's was barely afloat on a tide of debt.

Jimmy began to take a closer interest in proceedings when Arnold Catesby was present. He had been co-opted to the board by the Ravens and it was apparent to Jimmy that he had a mission not entirely in line with the continued operation of St Edith's. The man was mesmeric in his ability to gain attention, although Jimmy had some difficulty in understanding what he meant. Hassett wriggled with enthusiasm and the Ravens fawned upon him. The locals looked at Catesby as though he was a mysterious creature dredged up from the depths of the sea, despite being immaculate and sweet-smelling in his City pinstripe.

"How about Catesby?" Jimmy had asked Toby Friabin.

"Catesby, my boy, is the stuff of old England. A paid-up member of the establishment. Public school, Oxbridge, law partnership in the City, financier, adviser to government on you-name-it, heading like a rocket toward a place in the Lords. Forget that he arrived on the island aged six, with an unpronounceable name, from the murk of Romania. Presumably with parents bearing money-bags. A cunning survivor of a series of financial disasters in the City. Marvellous knack of dodging the fallout. He is the man who governs us and will govern us more mightily yet."

Catesby had been a lawyer, a senior partner in a large City practice, and he retained in his dealings with the board, all the finnicky precision of a lawyer both in his speech, the movement of his hands and his deployment of his notes, which he held as though they contained holy writ. Holding a paper almost at arm's length before him, he would suddenly look up sharply at the audience and scan their faces with an expression which said: 'There, you see? That clinches it.'

He had a shining, hairless, olive-skinned brow, a beaked nose and a brooding Eastern European stare. In contrast, his voice was fruity and ripe. If you closed your eyes, you could think you were listening to an aristocratic, blue-eyed fop. Catesby was important, dignified, wealthy and used to considerable deference. He was entirely without a sense of humour. In his wordy, fiddling way, he had made a proposition about St Edith's buildings, which he pressed at a number of meetings. Jimmy did not quite understand it and Kate opposed. The Ravens purred as though they had received penetrating insights. The locals tried to stifle their yawns.

Toby was a steady ally of Kate's on the Board, but he liked to think of himself as the peacemaker between the Ravens and the locals. He was easy and unselfconscious with the Ravens. He appeared not to envy them, but merely to regard them as different. "Went to a different reform school than me, didn't they?" he said to Jimmy.

Toby had given Jimmy some unflattering vignettes of other members of the board. "Hassett's a little tit. Member of the parish council in Little Didbury, or wherever, church on Sundays and very competent at charging aged gents for losing a good part of their fortunes on the stock exchange. Crumlin, thirty years a schoolteacher of boys. His biggest experience of life is a Boy Scout camp. Occasionally, he'll step out of line and support Kate. Rollinson, the headmaster of Ravensthorpe, a sanctimonious so-and-so. Fergus Montfort, the art dealer, very crafty, very rich and a good man to give you lessons on how to beat the Revenue."

At one recent meeting, all the board members had taken their seats except Catesby and Kate who were conferring in her office. Duncan Hassett ruled that they would wait. They stared at each other frigidly, implicitly rejecting small-talk. Fergus Montfort, no respecter of protocol, asked, "What's this letter from one of the minions of the Bishop of Southwark about the church?"

St Edith's used a strip of land as a right-of-way to their other building; the right of way passed the door of one of the diocese's functioning churches.

"The Bishop's saying we're barring the use of the church for worship. Not true of course. I have Kate's assurance." Hassett sat back confidently.

"She's a Buddhist, so what can you expect?" Crumlin sneered.

"We shouldn't have a Buddhist director." Montfort, more interested in past mistakes, said.

"We didn't know she was!" Crumlin's hand in Kate's appointment made him defensive.

"That's your negligence and naivety," Montfort teased. "Imagine employing the director of a Christian settlement and then finding out afterwards that she's a Buddhist. It beggars belief!" Montfort's manner almost hid his contempt.

"You can't just ask people point blank," Hassett said, taking up the defence of the interview panel, which he had chaired.

"You can frame a question that gets it out, like, 'Do you ever worship at Southwark Cathedral?'" Montfort said.

Hassett's red nose was burning. "Kate Martin's background is very... she went to Roedean for God's sake!"

"The daughters of successful hauliers, bookies and cleaning contractors all go to Roedean," Crumlin said.

Montfort sighed theatrically, "You were suckered..."

"Kate never concealed anything, it's just that..." Hassett groaned.

"It's just that the interview panel was inept," Montfort said.

"Now that's... what has it got to do with the use of the church anyway?" Hassett asked.

"She'll close it down, lock it up," Montfort said.

"Can't do that. Ecclesiastical Law," Crumlin said.

"No, you can't put a catch on a church lavatory door without an order from the Archbishop," Hassett agreed.

"But she can... she will, and she is!" Montfort spat out the words lightly.

"What's wrong with a Buddhist?" Jimmy asked.

Hubert Sloan turned and glowered at Jimmy's impertinent interjection. "A person who wears an orange robe and meditates all day?"

"It doesn't sound so bad," Jimmy said.

"It's a nasty foreign practice to have in a Christian settlement," Sloan said.

"Kate doesn't wear an orange robe, does she?"

"Look, Jimmy," Sloan said, "I think you could expand your knowledge a little. Can I suggest an adult education course? Seriously, a lot of young people nowadays find it's a good way to…"

"Keep outta trouble?"

"Catch up with their education."

Kate and Catesby entered the meeting.

7

The Butchers' Row killing did not excite much public attention; the murder of a prostitute. The newspapers gave it a brief mention; the television stations ignored it. The case occurred at a time when the Metropolitan Police were under more pressure for national security than usual and it was assigned to Chief Inspector Dan Hamish. He had spent ten year years of his career in the murder squad and the remainder with the fraud squad. He was planning to retire in six months' time. He would be supported by a forensic team from Scotland Yard and local know-how from the Jarndyce Street station in Southwark.

Hamish appeared willing to accept the task, as he always did, but it was unwelcome. He had become used to the sedate pace and comparative absence of histrionics in fraud work. In contrast, all murders were sad and sordid and that of a prostitute, which often involved psychopathic issues, he found depressing; he had these feelings even after his years of such work. He had had a steady career and now he was looking forward to enjoying his pension with his wife; following interests that had become more real to him than police work: gardening, butterfly conservation, walking and camping. He was a fit, lean, fifty-nine.

Dan Hamish's career in criminal investigation was, he had to accept, respectable rather than distinguished. He joined the police for a secure and reputable job, not because he had any ambition to be a cop. He was recognized, when he enlisted with his third-class degree in geography from Swansea University, as thoughtful and intelligent. The path to detective work soon opened. He took it because the police establishment was pleased with him and encouraged him. He didn't quite know what he was getting into. His service record reflected his reaction. He had never been highly commended for any of his work, but equally he had never been disciplined. Descriptions like 'solid', 'reliable', 'good-tempered', and 'safe' studded his personnel reports. He was popular with his peers. The fact that he was an unchallenging colleague and moderately competent had assisted his rise to chief inspector. But he had known for years that he would go no further and he did not wish to. He had, in the estimation of his superiors, no 'steel' in him, no 'bite', no 'cutting edge', no 'zeal', or any of the other similar epithets which are expected in the description of a top cop.

Hamish handled his work in a distant, dispassionate way, like a scientist handling dangerous bacteria; he was very cautious. He had come to view detective work as walking a tightrope between the lawful and the criminal. He had seen more able colleagues fall, sometimes not really aware of the pit that awaited.

He had worked with plenty of detectives who were hawkish. They wanted to *get* the person who could be charged and convicted. They were competitive with their colleagues and combative with the law-breaker. It was a contest. They intended to win. They wanted to chalk up a successful score sheet. Hamish thought this attitude suffused the detective force the more experience they gained. And it began to show in their cracked and broken faces. They sometimes looked and behaved like their prey. You mightn't have believed them if they said they were passionate about pursuing justice. What they were passionate about was the combat. To achieve their ends, they would take shortcuts – change the date on a letter, fail to record a witness statement accurately, make a false entry in their notebook, tell a lie when it was somebody's word against theirs, kick a suspect around the room. Their activities had been circumscribed by closed circuit television, complaints procedures, and the ubiquitous cameras and recorders, but the nature of their operations never changed: it was right up to the edge, and over it a little. And some of them fell, heavily.

Hamish didn't mind working with such officers. They weren't evil people. It was human nature to be toughened by combat. They were like commandos. He personally abstained from violence, lies and petty manipulations not because he was morally above these tricks, but because he had the imagination to anticipate the trouble he might cause himself if he was discovered. Hamish didn't care enough about winning to want that additional advantage. He didn't regard himself as superior to the commandos. In truth, he knew he was somewhat handicapped. He wasn't as effective at his job as he could be. There was something in his nature which made him stand off the issues without emotion and above all with self-protection in mind.

Hamish was at Pew Street at 7am and directed to the third floor. He rapped on the door and heard the occupant scuffling around. He also thought he heard the high note of a woman's voice. He made no attempt to enter but waited until the door was opened.

"Chief Inspector Hamish, CID. You're James Morton?"

He saw a tousled youth in bare feet, t-shirt and jeans, meanly nourished and pale. He proffered his ID. Jimmy eased out though the doorway and closed the door behind him. He looked carefully at the ID; they stood silently in the bare passage while he did this.

"I'm investigating the murder of Magdalena Walecka," Hamish said. "I want to ask you a few questions." He spoke in a quiet, serious voice.

"I already answered questions for Chief Inspector Sneed," Jimmy said, promoting Sneed to a higher rank. Hamish was amused.

"There'll be quite a lot of questions from both of us while we're investigating. Anywhere we can sit down, Mr Morton?"

"I only got one chair."

"Well, we can talk here for the moment. The police pathologist says Magdalena, Eva, had very rough intercourse consistent with rape and was sodomised before she was strangled. Did you know that?"

"I don't know nothin' about it."

"But you've already told Mr Sneed that you were called to view the body in Mrs Thrussell's flat. So, you do know something."

"That's all I know."

"But Mrs Thrussell says the body was never in her flat."

"She asked me to help her move the body out of her flat."

"The body was found at the end of the hall by the door of the apartment where Eva lived with Johan Tomachek. So Mrs Thrussell moved it without your help?"

"I never put it there. I never touched it."

"Why would Mrs Thrussell tell a lie?"

Jimmy had a slight, sarcastic smile. "It's bleedin' obvious."

"Mmmm. How could the body have got there, Mr Morton?"

"I don't know." He wasn't going to mention Kevin Thrussell. His code was not to crap on anybody, unless he had to save himself.

"Let's leave that for the moment. Gloria Thrussell says she was at a party over the road at the Dog & Duck public house the night Eva died and Eva was there. Were you?"

"No." Jimmy was emphatic.

"You were never in that building that night?"

"I never went to the party. I never knew there was a party until I got there to clean up about midnight."

"Was anybody else there when you went to clean up?"

Jimmy hesitated. He had agreed what they would say with Toby. "I was with Toby Friabin. He asked me to help clean up."

"When?"

"I'd come back from Betty's. I was goin' to bed."

"A last-minute arrangement. Why clean up at that hour?"

"I dunno. Toby asked me."

"Suspicious, isn't it? Could be the cleansing of a crime scene. Were you paid?"

"Naah. He asked me to help."

"Wasn't it unusual to call on you at this late hour?"

"No. Toby's my boss – one of my bosses."

"I'm glad you told me you were there, at the Dog & Duck, Mr Morton. We've collected a large number of prints from the rooms and we'll want to match them up. One of my people will get your prints later today. I expect we'll find you're in our collection from the rooms. Who was at the party?"

"I dunno. I told'ya I wasn't there. I gotta go downstairs and help with breakfast."

"I haven't finished yet. We've found traces of heroin and cocaine in the rooms. Do you ever use them?"

"Naah. I'm clean."

"Did you see heroin or cocaine in the rooms when you were cleaning up?"

"Too valuable to leave around, innit?" Jimmy couldn't resist a grin.

"Could you answer the question? I'm talking about powder, papers, needles, that stuff." Hamish had a benign look.

Jimmy was wary. "Naah. There was a mess. Food. I didn't look. You already know."

"Don't go far away in the next few days, Mr Morton. We'll certainly need you for further questioning."

Hamish left Jimmy Morton thinking he was a remote suspect. He had already found that Morton had no record. An insubstantial youth with a clean record, like Morton, was not likely to have committed rape, sodomy and murder, but you could never tell. Morton seemed quite self-possessed to Hamish, who thought he recognized the type: rough, uneducated, probably quite bright, with a harsh background, but perky good humour. He had the cheeriness of people who hadn't much to be cheery about which always surprised him.

Hamish had developed the habit years before of cruising around the witnesses and the murder site when he started an investigation, avoiding in-depth interviews, attempting to get a picture of the crime, a sense of what probably happened. What concerned Hamish more than Morton's involvement was the party at the Dog & Duck. Gloria Thrussell had revealed not only Eva's presence but that of members of the board of St Edith's Settlement. She described her role as a hostess. When Hamish got the flavour of the boy's night out from her, he had lost no time in getting his forensic team to scour the premises.

Hamish attended a case conference at the Jarndyce Street Station with Turk and Sneed. They discussed their findings huddled round the coffee table in Turk's dingy office. "I called each of the board members who were at the party to tell them I'd want a statement," he said.

"And?" Turk had a cynical smile.

"Utter surprise. Couldn't understand why that could possibly be. Only too willing to cooperate. Exquisitely polite."

"What did you expect?" Turk was watching this import from the Yard who would call the shots on the case, carefully.

"Exactly that. Just going through the process," Hamish spoke airily.

"Big jocks," Sneed sniffed. "Be wary."

"Yeah, we could all be demoted." Turk laughed harshly.

"They want to cover their whoring," Sneed said.

"They'll fight," Turk said. "But we have a perfect target in Morton. Why worry?"

"I'm not so sure," Hamish muttered tonelessly.

"We've got to get sure. This case has got poisonous barbs all over it," Turk raised his voice. He opened his eyes wide and showed his white teeth unpleasantly.

Hamish was well aware that if he pressed Arnold Catesby and his companions as strongly as they deserved, there could be repercussions which could affect him personally. Turk wasn't wrong about the poisonous barbs.

"We'll see what we can get out of Gloria Thrussell, Peabody and Durbin," he said.

"Omerta," Sneed said, squashing that course. They all knew the rule of silence which tended to prevail where witnesses were involved in other illegal activities which might be revealed.

"Rita Durbin is a tough, professional sex worker. She won't give much,"Turk said.

"Friabin is a definite suspect," Hamish said. "He set up the party and cleaned up afterwards."

"He's a well-known guy around this manor. Must be late forties. Married. No record. I don't see him in the frame," Turk spoke gently and categorically.

Sneed agreed. "We're down to Morton or Kevin Thrussell."

"What about Tomachek, the pimp?" Hamish asked.

"Has an alibi. Checks out." Sneed was matter-of-fact. "Why would he kill the golden goose? The job was done by a customer. It's Morton or Thrussell."

"Could be one of the horde of vagrants got to her as she was crossing the road," Hamish said.

"Yeah. Find him."Turk dismissed the idea with a sniff.

Hamish floated another. "Emmett, the manager of the night shelter?"

"Could be a gay psychopath targeting a female prostitute, but I don't think so,"Turk said. "Present enquiries tend to show he never left St Edith's premises on the night. Tell me, Dan, what's your real feeling for the thing?" He leaned over toward Hamish, hungry for a reply.

"I think Eva was murdered at a sex party and her body dumped over the road."

"The forensics don't support a murder at the Dog," Sneed said quickly.

Turk erupted. "Right! Whatever other vileness was going on there, we'll get fucking well fried if we try to push that one!"

Hamish thought that Turk and Sneed, although on the face of it mismatched, were a neatly dovetailed pair: the dark, explosive Turk swaying over the shabby, runty, yellow-faced Sneed. They seemed to work together in lockstep, Bill and Ed, the demanding Turk and the sycophantic Sneed. They had one mind between them: to keep a clean nose and, Hamish suspected, a continuous flow of graft. They would make good characters in a novel or a film. They made him feel colourless. Yes, he was supposed to be chief navigator, but he only had a light hand on the tiller. The vessel would sail itself under the hands of Bill and Ed, and he could feel it.

Hamish was quite objective as police procedures brought up first one suspect and then another and circumstances pointed to A rather than B or C. It didn't make any difference to him if his intelligence told him that A was innocent. If there was a case against A, he would recommend prosecution of A. He had no concern about the outcome of conflicts of interest and power which swayed decisions to prosecute. Bribery and power pressure were just the animals in the woods that he had to safeguard himself against.

"OK, guys," he said gently, "but we better check out every angle first."

Turk and Sneed looked at each other, bulbous black eyes meeting sludgy grey ones. Hamish tried to read the signal. He thought it said 'We'll have to watch this quiet bastard from the Yard and steer him away from the Dog & Duck.' He enjoyed needling the pair. What they didn't realise was that they had nothing to fear from him.

8

Paul Emmett was a friend of Jimmy's. They frequently sat together under the porch of the shelter talking while they were watching their homeless customers. And sometimes when the homeless were settled in their beds, they went up to Paul's room which had two chairs and was more spacious than Jimmy's, and they talked for a while about the books that Paul had given Jimmy to read. They oiled the conversation with Paul's supply of whisky.

Jimmy had met Paul when he started to clean Number 10. And when Jimmy moved into his room at St Edith's, he awoke after a night of drinking and talking to find Paul in his bed. Before Paul could do anything, Jimmy had to say, 'I can't do this, Paul. I don't have any feelings about it.'

Paul was apologetic. There had been a misunderstanding. Jimmy had been partly responsible; it was the result of drink and loose talk about sex and friendship. But far from souring their relationship, the experience seemed to bring them closer together. Paul began to give Jimmy books to read and took on the occasional role of tutor.

One night when they were in Paul's room, Jimmy asked, "Whaddya think about Eva, Paul? I been gettin' heat over it."

"Eva's murder is… what happens," Paul replied depressively. "You're involved?"

"Not involved. I went over to Ma Thrussell's. Saw the body like I told you. And Toby and I cleaned up at the Dog

& Duck afterwards. Sneed had me in to the station. And now I had a visit from a tech at the Yard."

"You're already involved, boy. You ought to get out of here; it's a mire; we're all in it. I don't mean because of Eva. That cloud will probably pass."

"You includin' yourself in this get-out thing?"

"Sure. But I'll never go. You know my story. It's been all round the houses and it follows me like shit on my shoe wherever I go." He gulped his whisky and helped himself to another shot.

According to village gossip, when Paul was a young and dedicated Roman Catholic priest, ten years before, his superiors had been preparing to send him to a Jesuit college in Rome. A scandal with young boys had put an end to that. What precisely happened was never made clear by the chatter. Paul left the church for prison, sacrificed, he was said to have said, to save other priests.

His gratitude for Jimmy's pragmatic acceptance of him seemed immeasurable. Jimmy genuinely liked Paul and felt sorry for him; Paul was like a man with a painful, suppurating wound. But he also realized that Paul could help him. Paul was a scholar.

Jimmy couldn't think of an appropriate reply. After a silence, he said, "Did you try to… stop?"

Paul spoke without emphasis as though he was talking about somebody else. "After I started it I couldn't stop, regardless of my vows, regardless of the harm I knew I was doing the boys. It was like offering a starving man a steak. It was like an alcoholic craving liquor and finding it at his elbow."

Hearing this and watching Paul's taut face and staring eyes, Jimmy felt that *he* was a priest himself, receiving confession and ministering to a guilty person.

"Kate's not a misfit. She's straight up," Jimmy declared, slightly embarrassed and anxious to change the subject.

"We've all got a touch of rot, Jimmy. Every goddamn one of us. It's the human condition. Different degrees in different people and different communities, but …"

"Naah. Not Kate."

"You know about Kate?"

"What?"

"When Kate was appointed, she sent a circular letter to the board, staff and even some of the users saying how honoured she was to get the appointment." Paul paused.

"Sounds right to me," Jimmy said.

"I don't know whether sending that letter was a miscalculation on her part. It was certainly a deliberate act, and she's an intelligent and experienced woman."

"So, she was pleased to get the job."

"She said how proud she was as a Buddhist, to be appointed to head St Edith's, which had a past tradition of priest-directors. The tradition was abandoned long before Kate, for want of them. She promised in the letter to do everything to minister to all faiths and those with no faith, on a fair and equal basis."

Jimmy was confused. "I know she's a Buddhist. Sounds fair enough."

"Well it wasn't. I suppose the staff and users didn't care if she was a Scientologist or a Satanist, but I can tell you, the letter was received at board level not with mere startled surprise and perhaps distaste. Oh, no! The Ravens were spitting blood. They're always harking on about it, blaming each other for what happened."

"Yeah, I heard them bitching. It doesn't seem like a big deal to me. The Ravens employed her."

"Look at it this way, Jimmy. The Ravens thought they

were getting a middle-class Englishwoman, with a good university degree in sociology, devoted to community service. Kate's managed important projects for Tower Hamlets and Camden," Paul said, giving a rare, genuine laugh. "And here's the funny part. They *were* getting such a woman!"

"They don't have no beef, then."

"They had *assumed* that she was like them, at least a nominal Anglican or at worst, a practicing Roman Catholic. That would have been all right."

Jimmy laughed too. "They missed a trick. Whyn't they ask her?"

"Well, there's a limit to what you can ask. The Ravens' side of the board felt hoodwinked including Hassett who chaired the panel! But what could they say? Oh, dear, having *their* charity in the hands of a Buddhist! Wringing of hands. What, after all, is a Buddhist to these masters of the economy, except somebody with an obscure alien belief which they never expected to have to deal with in their whole lives!"

"Yeah, well, they're snobs," Jimmy said, thinking it was amusing.

"That's why you'll hear that Kate gets a rough ride from the board at times."

"I seen it."

"The Ravens can't understand why any white Englishwoman should be a Buddhist unless she's weird, and in this failed Church of England venture, a Buddhist boss grates on them. So, Kate's job is very edgy. She can get a gritty reception at meetings and there have been calls for her resignation."

"How do you really know, Paul?"

"Garnet Peabody takes the minutes."

"Are you saying Kate should have said she was a Buddhist?"

"She wouldn't have got the job."

"So, she kept quiet?"

"I guess she would say she wasn't asked so she didn't speak."

"Why do you think she mentioned it afterwards?"

"She was entitled to keep quiet but I think, having got the job, she wanted to stick her religion up the arse of the board members. Great! She ought to have known that they'd hate it. The other possibility is that she naively thought she was being up-front with everybody and that was a terrible miscalculation. The time for being up-front was when she was before the interview panel. I don't think Kate's naïve."

Jimmy thought about this and then with a grin said, "So it was deliberate. I reckon Kate's all right."

"Look, she is a big do-gooder who gets things done, but she has flaws. She overlooks St Bernard's for example."

"It's a neat scheme."

"It's fraud and you collect for it."

Jimmy bridled more readily after the whisky. "I ain't hurtin' nobody and neither is St Bernard's. I gotta pay my way."

"Of course you do."

"There's plenty of neat schemes, Paul. Shit, they're all round us."

"Sure. That's what I'm saying."

Nagged by his involvement in Eva's death, Jimmy went over to Butchers' Row to see Betty Thrussell after his stint in the City. He knocked at the heavy panel and Betty squinted through the spy hole and eventually opened the door. Her face was tear-stained.

"Whatcha want, Jimmy?"

"I thought I better come over and see you about Eva. Sneed had me into the station the other night and a new snoop from Scotland Yard saw me this morning."

"Oh, gawd, I'm worried," she said, backing her bulky hips away from the door to let him in. "Sneed's been here."

He followed her a few steps down the bare hall, its electric bulb hanging on a wire over the rug where Eva's body had rested, into the sitting room. The room was damp and smelled of boiled cabbage (not that Betty ever boiled cabbage); it was choked with a couch and greasy armchairs. On the walls were small pictures of fairytale houses and gardens in metal frames. Two teddy bears and a soft panda with a broken neck sat on a side table with a vase of paper flowers. Nothing much had changed since Jimmy used to board here.

A bulbous young woman with a mass of long blonde hair, her face slashed by two bleeding lines of lipstick, sat on a couch.

"Hiya, Gloria. How're the babies?"

"Little devils. Have a pew, Jimmy."

She seemed pleased to see him. Betty went to the kitchen to make tea.

"It's about Eva. I dunno what's goin' down and I don't want it," Jimmy said, settling in an armchair.

"Yeah. Mum and I was just talkin'. But whatsit to you?"

"I was here. Betty called me over. Eva's body was in the hall outside this door."

"Kevin moved the body into the corridor after you was here, Mum said."

Jimmy's habitually cheerful look had gone. "Betty told Sneed the body was *neve*r here."

Betty heard him from the doorway. "I didn't know what to say… I didn't mean anythin' 'gainst you."

Jimmy didn't rebuke her. She was a wreck. He thought

Kevin must have panicked after their meeting at the entrance to the flats and being seen with what Jimmy had guessed was a body bag. "Kevin'll have the cops on his tail."

"We won't be telling them," Gloria said. "We didn't tell Sneed nothin'."

"Except about me. They'll detect it if he touched her."

"We don't know what to do, Jimmy," Gloria said.

"What happened over at the Dog? You was there," he asked Gloria.

"You didn't tell me you was there," Betty said to her daughter.

"Yeah, I was there," Gloria said reluctantly. "Who told you, Jimmy?"

"The Yardy. An y' can't hide things like that anyway. A kid's dead. What happened?"

"It was a high-class party. All those St Edith's poofs, Hassett and all," Gloria said.

"Who else was there?"

"Garnet Peabody and another tart."

"What happened at the party? Garnet Peabody walked out; why?"

"Nothin' happened. I dunno what was in Garnet's head. And why are you askin' all the questions?"

"I don't want to be dragged in. Sneed an' the Yardy've already been at me."

"Why should you be dragged in?"

"Because Betty lied to Sneed."

"I didn't mean anythin' by it," Betty moaned. "Sneed doesn't know anythin' about the body being in this flat."

"Yes he does," Jimmy said, "because I told him the honest truth. Y'see how things get screwed up? I told you to leave the body alone and call the police."

"I'm worried about Kevin," Betty said.

"Did Kevin do this?"

"Don't say a thing like that, Jimmy!" Betty squealed.

"Kevin wasn't around," Gloria said. "He just came back and helped Mum shift the body into the corridor."

Jimmy realized that it was too much of a coincidence for Kevin to have 'come back' from nowhere, but he didn't comment.

"Who was the other girl at the party, Gloria?"

"Rita Durbin. One of Toby Friabin's bitches."

"Rita. I've heard the name around. Toby tried to tell me you and Garnet were the only ones."

"Listen, Jimmy, I told Sneed it was an ordinary party. He asked me when I last saw Eva. I told him at the party. She was OK when I left." She hesitated and screwed up her red lips. "Although maybe she wasn't."

"You mean something might have happened that you didn't see."

"'Spossible."

"And Sneed bought your story?"

"Sure," Gloria said confidently.

"You offer to tickle his willy?"

Gloria gave her version of a mysterious smile. "We women have our ways!"

Jimmy went back to Number 10 Pew Street and told Toby what he had learned.

Toby said, "Those dear ladies will turn back-flips to protect lovely Kevin. I had Catesby on my back today. He called in here personally on the pretext of board business. I said that there was no way I could conceal the fact that he and his brave companions were at the Dog & Duck because Mother Thrussell blabbed about your intervention, raising the question where the body had come from and whither it was bound."

"I didn't intervene in nothin' Toby. I told her to leave the body and call the police and I told the police exactly where the body was when I saw it. Them Ravens commit murder and it's my fault?"

"No, it's events dear boy, as the great Harold Macmillan once said. The inevitable chain of accidental consequences. Master Catesby was not best pleased."

"The cops would have got on to them anyway."

"I have, myself, had a visit from the estimable Chief Inspector Hamish, who carefully noted what I said about the attendance at the party and our little effort afterwards. Our good friend Sneed was in attendance, attempting to persuade Hamish that I am a pillar of society."

"You had no alternative but to talk about the party, Toby. The cops have got the prints of all of us. Catesby & Co.'ll be wrigglin when Hamish nails them. I mean what're they goin' to say? It was a party with whores, an' one of them was worked over an' killed. No gi'ttin' away from that."

"My boy, your faith in some facts is touching. Do not underestimate the skill and cunning of the St Edith's gentlemen in, shall we say, rearranging the facts, bringing other facts to the fore deserving of more attention. And do not underestimate the servility of our loyal men in dark suits when confronting power. The good Hamish will doff his cap and retreat out of the door backwards."

"Do you reckon?"

"No, Jimmy. I don't reckon. I'm certain. Our grand gentlemen will not be implicated in this nasty business in any way at all, unless something very strange happens. Like a visitation from another planet."

"They can commit murder and get away with it?"

"Murder is dangerous, like an unexploded bomb, but yes, they can. Nothing is beyond the ingenuity and influence of Milord Arnold."

9

One of Jimmy's regular pitches was Borough Market. He worked the fringe of the crowd quietly for a few hours one market day a week. He usually made his 'stand' near the local authority notice board under the arches. He took the time to scan the board, to see whether there were any jobs, or events that might interest him. He was working toward the idea of another job, but nothing was quite as lucrative, or gave him as much time to himself, as being one of Toby's collectors and a part-time helper at St Edith's. A costly factor was housing. He would have to get his own room if he moved. However, it was interesting to browse the notices and speculate. He usually ended his study with the police notices asking for help with crimes or motor accidents.

On this occasion, it was a missing persons' poster that he particularly noticed. He habitually scanned the police list of missing and wanted persons at the shelter. Paul received a copy from the Jarndyce Street station. Sometimes he or Jimmy or one of the other trusties identified somebody from the list. Paul didn't necessarily report the wanted person to the police. He talked to them first and sometimes persuaded them to go to the Social Services office. Sometimes he did nothing. The photos on the police sheet at the shelter were small and smudged. The photograph on the notice board of the missing girl, Martine Cleland, was larger and there was a lot of detail. The face was familiar.

She was described as a twenty-year-old missing from a clinic. The way the notice was worded implied, but didn't specifically say, that the clinic was a secure place where she was under treatment. You had to assume that the treatment would be for drug rehab or mental problems. She was wanted by the police for questioning in connection with an assault. The date given was the date 'Joe', now 'Josie', arrived at St Edith's. The photograph of Martine looked like it had been done at a studio. She had long, dark, wavy hair, glistening lips and airbrushed satin skin. Jimmy thought it was nevertheless Josie, who wore no makeup, had short brown hair with fair tufts and pimples on her cheeks.

Jimmy and Josie had worked their morning patch and retired for lunch in a cheap and crowded restaurant off the market. They crouched, almost head to head, over a small table, buffeted by people moving past them to get in or out of the premises. When the plates were set in front of them and their eyes were off each other, looking down at the mess of bangers and mash floating in brown gravy, Josie said, "What's got into you today? You've hardly said a word."

He brought up his head to look straight at her. "Martine Cleland."

She jumped nervously, put down her knife and fork slowly and folded her arms, having already declared that she was ravenous. "OK, you've got me. How did you find out?" Her eyes were pale grey and rather small. Lines appeared on her forehead and round her tight mouth. The lips were thin, bloodless.

"There's a missin' persons' notice on the board at the market. Your name'll probably appear on the police sheet at the shelter, too."

"Oh, hell. Anybody could grab me!"

"I don't think so." He stopped abruptly. Silence, into which rushed the clamour of the diners.

"What are you going to do about it?" She had a note of alarm in her voice.

"Depends on your game. All that crap about havin' your money lifted by a girlfriend."

"What do you expect me to say? I just escaped from a high-security clinic? I'm a nutter on the run? What?" Her indignation had a screechy edge.

He considered and returned to what he thought was the main point: "Have you had a detox?"

"Yeah, I said so. But it was at the clinic."

"Can you handle it?" He was sceptical and knew you couldn't believe a junkie.

"I think so… I'm a bit wobbly."

That, he thought, was probably honest. "There's plenty of stuff floatin' around here. You can be back on the hook just like that."

"Yeah, I know. I'm going to try. And I don't have any money, do I?"

"I'm payin' you fair. But no, you don't have money – for that. *Are* you a nutter on the run? Whyn't you just behave yourself and get cured?" His voice had no strand of sympathy; it was business-like.

"I want to find out what my stepfather is doing. He put me in the clinic. I haven't been sectioned, or anything like that."

"Your stepfather? What's he got to do with it?"

"A man named Catesby."

Jimmy had years of cultivating a poker face to deal with his fortunes, so he showed no surprise. But he was surprised. Was it another yarn? He gave himself a mark for realising she was a phony. And there had to be a story behind it. "Arnold Catesby is on the board of management of St Edith's," he said quietly.

"I know. Or rather I knew he was tied up in some way with what's going on down here. You've heard of him? He's a very big piece of shit." She said the words as though they tasted bad.

"I'm a user-rep on the board… He goes on and on at meetings. Thinks he's Christmas."

"You actually know him? God, I can't *believe* that." Her voice hit a high note.

"No, y' wouldn't expect a small piece like me to know a big piece, would ya'?"

"I didn't mean it that way, Jimmy."

"And I don't know him. I sit with a few other little turds and listen to him warble."

"What does he say?"

"I dunno. I never pay much attention. Anyway, why you on the run?" He was determined get the whole story.

"Because he wants to diddle me out of my share in my father's estate."

"He puts you in a clinic because you're an addict. That's where you should be. You run away. What happens next?"

"So, he's my stepfather and the court appointed trustee of my interest in my father's estate. Get it? While I'm inside, he's in control."

"Is that a big deal?"

"It is to me. It's about land my father left me."

"What about the nutter thing?"

"He wants to get me sectioned. Then he's home and dry. He doesn't need to bother about me."

"Why come here, to St Edith's. Whyn't take your bellyache to a lawyer?"

"Because I know this place and I hadn't any money and needed a bed. I knew about the place years ago from my father. When he was alive, he was a donor. He was a Ravensthorpe Old Boy. I didn't have a friend to turn to, because the friends I have, or had, don't want to be tied up with a junkie. They're all right people. I guess I kinda scare them."

Jimmy too laid down his knife and fork, trying to sum the story up. It was beginning to sound as though it could be true.

"I'll ask you again, Jimmy, what are you going to do?" She was talking like he had a duty to act.

He took a long pause. He liked her. She was interesting. But she didn't mean anything to him. He didn't owe her. "Nuthin'."

"I can stay? Catesby will have private dicks on the case. I don't think they'll look for me at St Edith's Shelter."

"Sure. I guess you're as safe here as anywhere. Now that I know the story. Stupid of you to keep Butch. A dead giveaway."

"I love him. You don't understand. He's the only thing I have…"

"Keep him, then. Your risk, not mine," he said, lightly. "How'd you get hold of the dog anyway, if you were locked up?"

"It was a private clinic. They used to let me play with Butch in the garden. Catesby bought him."

"What's eatin' Catesby?"

"Money, fame, power, what else is there?"

"He's broke?"

"Never. He's loaded. A lot of it stolen from my father."

"So, what does he want if he's got plenty?"

She moved her eyes skyward and a small dimple appeared in her cheek as though he was being stupid. "You can never have enough money or fame or power, Jimmy. You always want more. Don't you know that?"

He smiled sourly. "If you don't have nothin', you don't need much to be satisfied."

"Catesby wants to erect a huge building, the tallest in Europe. This is a prize position, close to London Bridge. He'll produce beautiful plans and graphics and let most of the floors while it's on the drawing board and then build it. Little risk. Make a bomb."

"Sounds easy," Jimmy admitted.

"If you've got the land and planning permission and a big reputation to jack up loans, it is easy."

"Has Catesby?"

"He can raise the finance, I'm sure. But he hasn't got the land or the planning permission – yet. The land is in my father's estate."

"How come you know all this? Like what his plans are?"

"There was a time before I ran away that he told me."

"You gotta do business with him?"

"Yeah. I'd rather deal with a snake but it's unavoidable – if I get out of this fix I'm in."

"But where you goin' with this now?"

"I'm twenty-one in a few months. Then it's mostly mine unless I'm sectioned."

"What if Catesby moves before?"

"I think he's moving now in ways I don't understand. I don't know what I'll do. You see, anybody I might run to, lawyers, bankers, that lot, have already had an earful from Catesby that I'm crazy. The first thing they'll do is call Catesby. He's a big man. Well respected. And he'll say I'm barmy and send a doctor."

"But doctors can't just pack you off to the looney bin because somebody asks them to."

"True, but while Catesby is paying them plenty, and yowling about his concern for my health, and with my history of addiction, they'll take a long look at the case. I'll have to be placed under observation. Time will go by."

"What about the cops?"

"Another problem. I clocked a male nurse to get out of the clinic. Had to. I planned to get away unnoticed. But these things don't work out, do they? I doubt that I hurt him much. I couldn't have got away otherwise."

He was fairly sure that he was getting the true story this time. "I don't think it's the crime of the century; it just makes it easier to get the cops' support in trackin' you down. And it makes you look more wacky."

"What do you think, Jimmy?" She was crestfallen, punctured, perhaps realising her scheming was hopeless. Her hands trembled.

"I don't think you're crazy, but you certainly got a neat problem." He picked up his knife and fork and said in an objective, fatherly way, "C'mon, eat up girl, we'll find someone to look after the dog and we'll catch a movie."

10

Jimmy arrived at the hall of the Worshipful Company of Silversmiths, in Lark Lane, on the eve of the wine-tasting. He had the wine in the back of a truck provided by Toby. This was in preparation for St Edith's annual fundraising event. The Freemen of the Company, some of whom were ex-Ravens, were pleased to make their premises available at a reduced fee. He was admitted by a fussy attendant who didn't seriously believe Jimmy was from St Edith's until he had phoned Kate Martin.

Jimmy's task was to deliver, stack and arrange the wine and report anything to Kate that might need attention. In the hall, he was confronted by a vast cave of treasures: glistening chandeliers, frescoed walls, Grecian columns, tall gilt doors and life-sized oil portraits of the grandees of earlier centuries. He learned that here, the fortunate silversmiths of the City had regulated their affairs since 1327 with a Royal Charter from Edward III. Jimmy thought that they had drunk and eaten well, entertained useful people like the Lord Mayor and plotted and planned to guard their exclusive market.

However, even markets crumble and there was money to be made in letting these exclusive chambers. Tonight would see St Edith's guests, the prosperous and personable of many businesses and professions, enjoying themselves.

Jimmy laboured stacking dozens of crates of vintage wine along one wall. He ensured that the different labels were separated and had adequate tables near them with supplies of glasses and jugs for water. And discreet buckets. Chairs and lounges were scattered nearby.

The prelude to this delivery had been somewhat unusual for Jimmy. Twenty dozen boxes of expensive vintage wine, carefully selected by the board members, were ordered from a wine merchant and delivered to a store, provided by Toby Friabin at his car sales-yard. At the same time, twenty dozen boxes of various supermarket wines, carefully selected by Toby were also delivered. Jimmy was invited to remove the labels from all the supermarket wines and re-label them with the vintage labels which Toby had acquired, taking care to match the label to the type of wine.

When Jimmy questioned the authenticity of the labels, Toby, as was his way, deliberately misunderstood the question. "These labels are works of art," he said. "The man that did this can do passports and he has had experience doing twenty pound notes, so a wine label isn't much of a challenge."

"Y'reckon the people *tastin'* won't know it's only supermarket wine?"

"It's very good supermarket wine. I always drink it myself. And what will the punters know after a few tipples?"

"Maybe they can taste a nasty and won't want to order any wine."

Toby was undisturbed. "Blame the bottle. And who cares? St Edith's makes its money on the entry tickets and the raffles. If you win a case of wine, lucky you. Good supermarket wine. Retails for ten or fifteen quid a bottle. Wine fanciers are ordinary punters. Tell them a good story James, and they'll believe it; they'll believe anything. You just have to tell them authoritatively. Remember the Froggie's story that wine didn't travel from South America? Sounds rather possible when you're talking about those backward ex-colonies, what? And those crude Aussies spoiling their cheapo wine by putting screw caps on? Lovely bollocks, but well and truly believed – for a while."

"What's going to happen to the real vintage stuff you've got here?" Jimmy liked to get to the bottom of it.

"Sold to a friend of mine with a small wineshop at a very good price for him."

"What about the delivery orders you take at the wine-tasting?"

"We'll buy in the additional supermarket wine, change the labels to vintage and collect vintage prices."

"You don't have any kinda thought about this, Toby?" Jimmy prodded gently.

"Conscience? Guilt? Those luxuries? No, dear boy, not a simple man like me. Why should I? They prey on us. We prey on them. It's a game."

Jimmy didn't ask about the net proceeds, but guessed that the 'Toby Bank' was fairly flush.

Dressed in a plain grey, ready-made suit from the market, with a white nylon shirt and a red polyester tie, Jimmy attended the event. At first glance he looked smart. But he did not look quite right with shabby trainers on his feet, his only shoes. He could well have afforded a pair of black moccasins, but he was tight with money. And where would he wear them afterwards? As he was approaching the herd of guests, most of them from the City, he met Duncan Hassett prowling around the outskirts, looking for hands to shake. Hassett lifted his pink nose as though there was a bad smell and said, "I like your footwear, Jimmy."

Jimmy headed for the tasting tables hoping to hear the verdict of those who tasted the supermarket wine. He watched and listened. The tasters looked surprised at first sniff, but soon smiled and after much swishing and not very much spitting out, pronounced such phrases as 'rough but interesting', 'startlingly candid but catching', or 'having an after-taste of ripe plums', all the piffle he had read on wine labels. He noted that the comments were fanciful in proportion to the number of tastes, or rather slurps, that were taken. He thought that the gentlemen found it slightly disgusting to empty their mouths into a bucket and this could be avoided in a genteel way by swallowing. In the pressure of conviviality, orders for quantities of the wine were also being received and put aside to be completed later. Toby, today resplendent in a genuine tailored suit from Savile Row and snakeskin loafers (he told Jimmy), would see to that.

Jimmy saw Hubert Sloan with a thunderous face march briskly up to one of the tasters, Miles Cutforth. He could hear Sloan, who didn't trouble to keep his voice down, quite clearly.

"I don't know what's happening to St Edith's, Miles, but *that woman* will ruin us!" Sloan waved a sleeve with a protruding striped red and white double-cuff linked by heavy gold.

Cutforth half turned to deal with him with half his attention. The rest was on the ruby liquid he twirled in his glass. "I take it you mean Kate. What's wrong now? I mean more wrong than it was before."

"It's outrageous! I was talking to the MP here, Selwyn Frome, a yea sayer if ever there was one, and Kate Martin joined us, leading a nondescript young woman and saying she wanted to introduce her."

"The young woman?"

"No, the bloody waitress, Miles! Have you been tasting for long?"

"So who is she – the young woman?"

"She's Kate Martin's fucking *partner!* As cocky as you like, Kate Martin said, 'I'd like you to meet April Davis, my partner.' I damn nearly fell over. And do you know what that creep Frome said? He said, 'I've already had the pleasure. April's quite a high-powered lady in the Borough Council.' I was speechless!"

"Maybe when Kate said 'partner' she meant, you know, somebody she was working with," Cutforth smiled generously.

"Oh, get real, Miles. She meant this is the woman I fuck. The bloody nerve!"

"Yes, I suppose you've got to take it that way. We have a Buddhist *and* a lesbian as a director. That's… colourful… interesting, Hubert."

"Colourful. Interesting? It's disgusting. You, Miles and the rest of the panel were… I regard myself as broadminded, but what is happening is wrong. St Edith's should not be run by Buddhists or lesbians!"

"Kate Martin was *and is* outstanding." Cutforth blinked and rocked back on his heels helplessly.

"Arrrgh! Go back to your wine-imbibing, Miles!"

Hubert Sloan stalked away. Cutforth shrugged and returned to the tasting table. Jimmy heard it all.

Jimmy helped carry out trays of cakes and savouries from the kitchen and went around the guests, offering them. In the kitchen, he met Garnet Peabody who was also helping. He had known Garnet for a long time. He first knew her as a pupil from his fleeting appearances at school. She came from a big West Indian family. And she was a clerk at St Edith's.

When they both had a moment from their labours and the show was winding down, he edged her into a corner where they could talk.

"You were at the party the other night with Hassett? Enjoy yourself?" he asked.

"No I didn't, Jimmy. I left early… I hated performing in front of those pervs."

"What performance?"

"Pole dancing." She raised her eyebrows over her swelling brown eyes.

He nodded. "I thought you did a bit of that."

"Yeah. My act is quite nice. Artistic. Rhythmical."

"What made you leave?"

"After I'd performed, I had that bugger Catesby all over me. He thought he could do anything he wanted."

"What did you do?"

"Walked out, didn't I?"

"Eva was there?"

"Yeah. I'm not sure where she was when I went, but I saw her earlier. I'm sorry about what happened to her. I didn't like her much. She didn't use to speak to me. But still I think she didn't deserve what happened…"

"What did happen?" Jimmy asked, but he thought he heard a door close. Maybe it was just a sudden flicker of those big, tawny eyes.

"How would I know? I was outta there."

"Any other girls there apart from Eva?"

"Yeah…" she said reluctantly. "I better not say too much."

Jimmy understood the reluctance. He didn't press. "Whatcha doin' about it… what happened?"

"Nuthin'. Mindin' me own business," she said.

"Cops seen you?"

"Yeah. I told 'em what I told you."

"Did Catesby say anything afterwards, like at St Edith's."

"Apologised. Said he was sorry I left early. Gave me a hundred quid and squeezed my tit. He doesn't get it."

"What did you do?"

"Put the hundred quid in my purse, whaddya think? My additional fee for all the groping. But I already made a complaint to Kate about him coming into the office and grabbing my ass."

"This was before the party?"

"Oh, yeah, weeks, months. Happened a lot. He's always feelin' around, sticking his hands on my bum, wantin' me to go for a ride in his car. 'I got a lovely big, blue Bentley,' he says.'"

"You goin'?"

"No way."

"What's Kate doin' about your complaint?"

"She says she's talked to Catesby."

"What does she say he says?"

"Denies it. Kate says it's bad, but she says I can't get anywhere against such a big man without somebody else to say they seen it. And y'know it happens in private. He comes in the office when nobody's there."

"He's a cunning asshole."

"Yeah, but I got him!" Her eyes shone. Her anger was fueled up.

"Whaddya mean?"

"On camera. I'll make him a film star, him and his big prick!" She looked triumphant.

"Is it so big?" Masculine curiosity swerved him from his line of questioning.

"I ain't no expert, but it's bigger than my boyfriend's. To look at, I mean." Garnet chuckled playfully. "I shouldn'ta said that."

Garnet's boyfriend, Roland, was a promising black athlete.

"You *seen* it?"

Garnet grinned and nodded.

"Lemme get this straight. You filmed Catesby – at the party?"

"And his pals."

"Doin' what?"

"Havin' fun. Fuckin' and perving."

"Whyja do it?"

"Now why would I do that, Jimmy? My boyfriend is going to sell the film to a newspaper. We gonna get an agent. It'll be a proper deal. It'll serve that shithouse right."

"Shee-it! That's cool. Who fitted you with the camera? It's kinda technical."

"My boyfriend. He was pissed off at the guy groping me all the time. 'Get him,' he said."

"Wow! But won't it get all screwed up by the murder thing?"

"Yeah. You're right. That's what Roland says. We're figuring out how to play it."

11

Hamish called Catesby at his office in the City. He found it difficult to get through. He left his name and rank; Catesby responded very quickly. Apprehensions of the guilty, Hamish thought. When you get a call, it's not embarrassing for your secretary to jot down a police name and rank if your standing is unquestionable, but it's a speck of grit in the eye of the day.

Catesby came on to the line very strongly. "What is this, Inspector? We've already spoken." Very smooth, very genial, very dominating.

"It's a murder enquiry, sir, and I want to interview you about the party you attended last Saturday night in Southwark," Hamish said in an unemphatic formal voice.

"Oh, really?" Catesby sounded surprised as though he'd never heard of the murder. "I thought my driver must have parked my car in the wrong place. I can't imagine how I could possibly help."

"I think it would be better if we met, sir."

"By all means let's fix a date at my office." Catesby spoke lightly, indulgently.

"I'd prefer you called at the Yard, sir."

"I'd prefer you visited me here, Mr Hamish. We can be very private and relaxed here." Catesby still sounded as though he was gratifying a fanciful request.

In his time in the fraud squad, Hamish had interviewed many City men who were eloquent in their desire to help the police but insisted on being seen in their offices. It was always disturbing for a witness to report to a police station and it could be misunderstood by the curious. And the news media. Hamish granted the privilege without demur as he always had in the past.

A day later, he made his way to the fifth floor of a building on Lombard Street. He was guided behind a secretary over yards of highly polished teak flooring, past frosted glass and polished wood panelling; it was very quiet. Here, thoughts were generated in the softness of brains and transferred silently to electronic mail. The secretary swung open the unnecessarily tall doors of Catesby's office. The man rose from his desk at the end of the thickly carpeted room lined with law reports and directories. He lunged forward affably, his forehead shining, right arm extended.

In the few seconds of greeting, Hamish was confronted by the large eyes with their dilated pupils riding above the shining nose, a bulky, suited body a few inches shorter than his, and a small white hand. He was directed to an armchair slightly facing the floor to ceiling windows. The view showed the spectacularly intricate spires of churches of the seventeenth and eighteenth centuries, striving, where they could, to rise above the tide of glass and steel. Catesby took an adjoining armchair similarly inclined. Hamish regretted the arrangement instantly. He preferred to have his target in full sight, face-on.

He made no comment, but said, "Do you mind, sir, if I tape our meeting. It saves me taking notes."

"I expected it, Inspector. But first, let's have coffee."

The coffee arrived quickly while Hamish was arranging his recorder. Catesby asked him about his career in the force, and complemented the chat by referring to his own career in a mock-modest tone. The two paths were very unlike, but similar. One man was Acton Comprehensive, Swansea

University and the Metropolitan Police which Hamish thought of as a horizontal path. The other man was Radley, Oxford, the legal profession, big business and generous non-executive directorships, a splendid upward trajectory.

Hamish, not put down in the least by Catesby's patronising politeness, went on as quickly as he could, referring to Eva's fate, the pathologist's findings, and Catesby's rights.

"I'm very well aware of my rights, Inspector. I only hope you're not going to infringe them," Catesby said, haughtily.

"I want to ask you about your whereabouts on the night Eva was murdered," Hamish said.

"Inspector, I know nothing whatsoever about this and I know nothing of a girl you tell me is called Eva Walecka," Catesby recited with the studied sincerity of a play-actor.

Hamish had to turn his head awkwardly to see whether he had ruffled the parchment brow; but no, it was serene. "Ever seen her?" he asked, producing a photograph.

Catesby pushed the photograph aside with hardly a glance. "I've already told you, Inspector." More crisply now.

"I have to ask the questions, sir, if we are going to solve the case."

"Can I say, Inspector, that you are approaching this as though I was a murder suspect and I deeply resent that. It's insulting." A note of righteousness.

"I had no intention to offend, sir," Hamish replied in a soft, unemotional monotone.

"You have told me that Miss Walecka's body was found in a tenement in a street with a vile name in Southwark. I can assure you I have never been in a tenement in Southwark at any time in my life!" The voice now raised slightly and contemptuous.

"There is evidence that Eva was at a public house

nearby, the Dog & Duck, the same night. Were you in a private room at that pub that night, sir?"

"I'm not prepared to talk about my private affairs unless I can understand that there is meaningful information I can give you."

"I'd prefer you to answer my question, sir, which is certainly meaningful – whether you were in a private room at the Dog & Duck public house at the same time as Eva Walecka who was later murdered."

Catesby winced as though he was in pain. "I'd prefer *you* to give me further information about your enquiries."

"I'll take it you're refusing to answer, sir." Hamish was matter of fact.

"No, I'm not refusing, but I'm not going to answer questions in the dark about my private affairs."

Hamish shook his head with the crease of a smile around his mouth. "Well, we can't proceed in that way, you questioning me. As the investigation proceeds sir, I may have enough evidence to arrest you for questioning. If I do that, the arrest may become public."

"You are threatening me and you cannot conceivably have any justification for that…"

"You need to think about it, sir…"

"And you need to remember that I may sue you."

"I don't think we're getting anywhere," Hamish said, gathering up his recorder from the coffee table, good naturedly.

As he was going out of the door Catesby returned to his syrupy voice. "I'm sure you're going to find the person responsible for this crime, Inspector, without any recourse to me. But if I can help, please let me know. I don't doubt that we can have a meeting of minds."

Hamish merely pulled on a tight smile. He didn't

bother with repartee in such situations. As he descended in the elevator, he reflected that the interview had gone much as he expected. It followed a kind of pattern he was used to with such men. His fraud cases were peopled with wealthy businessmen's sweet words and denials. He had made precisely nil progress, but he had had an opportunity to size up Catesby. The man had an infectious energy and dominance; perhaps he was the 'leader' of the group at the Dog & Duck. He appreciated that Catesby was a clever manipulator of his own moods and reactions. His projected personality could be flexible with a repertoire of acts to meet any circumstances. He would never yield an inch in questioning. Would the time come when it was necessary to take Catesby in for questioning? Hamish knew he would have to tread carefully.

Hamish also went to Duncan Hassett's office in the busy Cheapside stockbroking firm of which he was senior partner. The dialogue about *where* they would meet was much the same as with Catesby and with the same result, although Hassett didn't have Catesby's composure. When Hamish was shown into his room Hassett quickly positioned himself behind his large and empty desk. Hamish set up the recorder and went through his preliminaries. Hassett was flushed and nervous with Hamish facing his distant quarry across a shiny surface of dark brown leather set in walnut.

"You were at the party at the Dog & Duck, Mr Hassett?"

"It was just a few drinks and a meal."

"Was Mr Catesby there, or Mr Crumlin, or Mr Montfort?"

Hassett didn't stop the calls on his phone, which gave him the opportunity to swivel his chair, his back to Hamish, pretend to a certain lack of attention and gain thinking time. "I'm not prepared, Inspector, to say who was there."

"Why? A few drinks and a meal. What harm is there in that?"

"It may sound schoolboyish Inspector, but I don't want you going to my colleagues and saying 'Duncan Hassett said so and so."

"But you were sober?"

"Yes. I had a few drinks."

"Were there drugs there?"

"Not as far as I know."

"You mean there might have been?"

"No I don't mean that. I never saw drugs. I don't touch drugs."

"And you left at what time?"

"About eleven."

"Was anybody else there, then?"

"Yes, as far as I remember."

"Girls?"

"I can't say."

"Mr Hassett, this is a murder enquiry. I'm going to ask you a very important question. Was Eva Walecka, the murdered girl, there?" Hamish produced the head-and-shoulders photo which had been obtained from Eva's room at Butchers' Row; it was in colour, faded, fuzzy. A wistful and pretty young woman.

"I can't say. I don't know Eva Walecka. There were several rooms. People were moving around," Hassett said, pushing away the photo.

"You mean she could have been there but you wouldn't know?"

"I can't say."

"Sir, Eva Walecka was cruelly murdered that night and she was a prostitute brought there for the pleasure of the diners, of which you were one, but you know nothing?"

Hassett was pale. His face had collapsed around his dominant nose, his eyes red. "Nothing."

"Are you saying you never had any sexual contact with any woman – or man – there?"

Hassett took another call. He swung back: "I had nothing to do with anybody sexually."

"Mr Hassett, we have evidence that all of the women there were sex workers in some form. Yet, you had none of this?"

"Nothing."

"I'm glad you admitted you were at least there, because we can establish that by other evidence."

"What evidence?"

"Both the young men who were your waiters have identified a photo of you taken from publicity material at St Edith's Settlement. We have fingerprints too. You'll appreciate that I know, or will know, by the same evidence, that Catesby, Crumlin, Montfort and others were also there."

"At least I never told you."

"May I say, sir, you shouldn't look at this enquiry in this way. This is a capital crime and we're looking for constructive help."

"I tell you, Inspector, it was a perfectly respectable occasion."

"Respectable with sex workers?"

Hassett didn't answer. Hamish said, "I'm not making a moral judgment about your gathering; I'd just like to get the facts."

Still no answer. "Why were you partying down in the docks area when you could have been at the Ritz?" Hamish pressed.

"Just because we chose to go to a place which is

five hundred yards from our boardroom doesn't make it suspicious." Hassett's voice was thin and quavery.

"Doesn't it, Mr Hassett? I'll be going now, but we'll meet again soon." He left Hassett propped in his chair, staring and seemingly paralysed.

Hamish had collected a lot of information about each of the witnesses. He appreciated that the sexual assault on Eva was not likely to be committed by a man with an otherwise exemplary sexual record. The chances were that the beast would have shown itself in some way at an earlier time. In the case of Catesby and his friends, he could find nothing on record. Catesby was a widower with an adopted daughter aged twenty. The daughter was a drug addict wanted by the police for a minor assault. She had absconded from a clinic. Hamish wanted to question her.

Hamish pursued a different line of enquiry because clean police records were simply the first port of call. How did Catesby behave with the women about him? He was the chairman of a successful hedge fund. It had a staff of financial experts and economists of about thirty, some of whom were women. Hamish had found that Catesby's fund had had its share of fairly high profile sex discrimination cases at employment tribunals; nothing surprising in that. It was the actual evidence and the persons directly involved in those cases that Hamish wanted to know about.

The normal practice for a City firm, if the discrimination and sexual abuse were blatant, would be for the woman to be paid off quickly and generously and even offered a reference, so Hamish only expected to uncover a scintilla of evidence of Catesby's predilections, if anything. But there were cases where the macho males in the fund evidently wanted to fight and there was a trial – and there *was* evidence.

He delegated the task of reading the evidence in the cases that had come to trial to an assistant who found Catesby directly involved in two. In the first case, a brave woman had won a big verdict. She spoke of a 'laddish' and crude mentality amongst the men. She claimed she had been propositioned and sexually fondled by Catesby and that there was a rule amongst the women (which was supported by another woman) not to be alone with him if possible. In the other case, which had been settled after being part heard, the allegations were more serious and amounted to rape but were obviously silenced a by a generous payment. These were not pretty findings but they didn't make Catesby a murderous psychopath.

He could find nothing similar in the past of the other St Edith's directors, but that didn't mean that they, or one of them, wasn't of the same ilk as Catesby. A possible route to verify whether there was a sexual predator amongst them would be to examine their personal computers and social network connections, but Hamish knew he would never get a warrant for that. He could have done it without authorization by hacking, but he made it a rule never to cross the red line.

Hamish was called in to see his superintendent a few days later. Superintendent Eric Webb was a benign superior, a former contemporary of Hamish's who had been promoted ahead of him. With their wives, they still occasionally made a foursome for dinner. Eric Webb inclined his silver head with a cordial greeting.

"Just a quick word, Dan. Something's come up on the Walecka killing. I'm not restraining your legitimate investigation in any way, but stay off Arnold Catesby and his fellow board members if you can. I'm sure they're innocent and want to help, but work around them if you can."

"I don't know whether they're innocent or guilty, Eric. You know the situation as well as I do. They profess a wish to help, but they don't want to."

"Perhaps that was because you put the frighteners on them, Dan."

"It's not me. They're worried men. They have a sex and drugs party. A prostitute is mauled and murdered."

"Do you have any evidence that the murder happened at the party?"

"Nothing conclusive yet. But it looks obvious."

"Dan, you know for them it's their reputations."

"I see, nothing criminal."

"Well, obviously not."

Hamish nodded silently and without any expression. "I understand, sir." He stood up, appending the 'sir' to show his friend that he was a soldier following orders.

As he was going out the door Webb came forward and took his arm. "These guys can make trouble for us, Dan. It's a matter of being a diplomat, that's all. No bars on your investigation, but…"

Hamish thought that being a cop and going where the investigation took him was ideal in the ethics manual. He and Webb inhabited a pragmatic sphere beyond that. He replied, "I'll be a diplomat, Eric, you can be sure of it. And no bars on the investigation." His statement was, as Eric Webb would have known, oxymoronic, but that was the order in which they worked. He would be, above all, a diplomat and the investigation would have to take care of itself.

"Thanks, Dan. We'll have to fix a meet soon. Gail mentioned only the other day how nice it would be to see you and Sarah again."

12

Some afternoons, when it was too cold to go on the street, after they had made love (as Josie called it), they lay in the narrow bed in Jimmy's room at Number 10 and talked. Jimmy made cups of instant coffee using the electric jug which sat on the floor by the door. He found Josie – he never called her Martine – as good a screw as he had ever had. He always sensed that although she too enjoyed herself, she was miles away. But perhaps he was the one who actually was. It was this distance on which he reflected when they were in the warmth of each other sipping their coffee. To him, she was like a Martian.

"You gotta hang-up about Catesby, Josie. I mean it's more than sex. OK, he made a pass. It happens."

"More than a pass. I'll tell you about it sometime, but sure as hell it's more than sex," she said. "Before this happened, I knew two things from my father. One was that Catesby was trying to push him out of their partnership. And the other was that he knew about Mom's affair with Catesby. He told me that once, when he was supposed to catch a plane and the meeting was cancelled when he got to the airport, he went home to find Catesby's car with its personalised number plate in the driveway. The pathetic thing about it was he didn't go inside. He went to a café and had a cup of coffee and a chocolate muffin and then rang home as if he was delayed at the airport. Typical of my father."

"But he changed his will."

"I think he always intended me to have his shares in the company. He didn't tell my mother. He always had the feeling that she didn't respect him. He was a decent man. The pull of Catesby was too strong for her. When he realised he was ill, he told me about Catesby. We were close. My mother was very bitter about the will, which was largely in my favour, after Dad's death. She didn't hide her feelings from me. I thought she had made her own hard luck. I didn't feel sorry for her. I always knew from my own observations that Catesby was on close terms with my mother. You know, you see things, little things in the school holidays. How a man greets a woman. Talks privately with her. Gives her covert gifts. I could feel the attraction between Catesby and my mother and I guess my father could too. Catesby and my mother married when Dad died. Soon after, I ran away from home. Hit the streets.

"Then my mother died, while having minor cosmetic surgery, presumably to make herself look more beautiful for Catesby. It was an awful accident. Catesby sued the ass off the surgeon and the anaesthetist. He got a pile of money from that and Catesby also got all my mother's property. She idolized him. But the point was that I was left the major share of Dad's estate. By this time I was an addict, sleeping on the street at times."

"Y' din't think of getting a job?"

"I was out of control. What would I do? I never learned anything at school and I had the drug habit."

"How did y' make out on the street?"

She laughed. "The usual way. Borrowing for keeps, stealing when I could and when I couldn't… selling it."

He was startled at her candour. He was also mildly repulsed. He had no claim on her, no right to expect that she had lived one sort of life rather than another, but it added to the distance between them. However, it wasn't going to stop him going to bed with her.

"I feel you've seen it all, Jimmy. You're not going to score me down."

Jimmy thought that was a big admission for any woman and it showed what she thought of him. Her pride didn't come into it. She didn't need or want to impress him.

"Uh-huh, selling it. Maybe just loaning it," Jimmy said lightly, trying to pass it off. He'd known girls, not full-time prostitutes, who sometimes sold the favours he could get for free and it hadn't meant anything to him. With Josie it *did* mean something.

"Sure, I just loaned my pussy around. I suppose a psychologist would say that the situation before my father's death, and the marriage of Catesby and my mother, were the cause of my addiction. I don't know. Life just seemed lonely and lousy, except when I had a buzz. Anyway, Catesby applied to the court to be appointed as my guardian. I was found and committed to the clinic under lock and key. I was too much out of my head to raise a finger to help myself."

"Maybe he was helping you. Stopping you from goin' completely down the tube."

"Sure. It looked like a decent and selfless act by Catesby. His real aim, I think, was to keep me in the nut house until I'd lost the will to manage my own life. I was fed a lot of drugs which I think effectively sedated me day and night, sapped my will and maintained my addiction. One small part of my brain began to appreciate this. I wasn't getting any better and I saw myself in that clinic for years. And consequently, I began to summon the will, through the clouds, to bust out of the place. For about three months I flushed a lot of the drugs down the toilet. I couldn't avoid all the drugs with doctors and nurses watching me but enough."

"Jesus, that's a bad scene. I didden' know doctors could do that."

"They can. If anybody questioned it the medicos would confront them with reports thicker than the Bible that everything done was therapeutic and proper and in my interest."

To Jimmy, Josie spoke from another existence. It touched on hate and greed which he knew about, but also upon things he read about in magazines and saw in the movies: a world of beautiful objects, cars and cabin-cruisers, holidays on Caribbean beaches, visits to exciting cities, and stays in luxury hotels. It was hardly a real existence to him and it made Josie seem unreal. That was one side of her life. It was difficult to think that her compact and shapely body had been available on the streets which he knew well. He feared the gutter too much to flop into it; he'd lived close to it all his life watching people submerge. But Josie had been there. And he wondered where she was now.

"So you didden' have a detox at the clinic?"

"No. I pulled myself together over a period of months, like I said."

"That's quite something."

"Anyway, that's enough about me. I'll tell you more about Catesby some time."

Jimmy had to reveal something of himself and the story of his life was very short and uneventful. The happenings *around* his life had been eventful, the poverty, the crime, the violence and drugs, but he had contrived to dodge them. Unlike Josie, who had travelled in Europe and the US, he had hardly been out of Southwark. The demands on his time to meet the skimpy needs of his life hadn't allowed it. He had never had a conventional holiday, or been north of Luton or south of Croydon. He'd always been too busy. He didn't feel he had missed anything, because he would make it up later. He'd travel in Spain and France and go to see the artists at work in Cornwall.

"The only home I really remember was the flat on Butchers' Row."

"That dump of derelict apartments across the patch?"

"Right. It wasn't as bad as it is now. It wasn't set for demolition. But it was pretty bad. Just Mum and me. I played around with the kids here. They used to bully me about the leg. 'Hoppy', 'limpy', all that stuff, getting around to punching and kicking. Kids would kill you, if you let them. I had to fight back, hard. After I'd blacked a few eyes and bloodied a few noses it got better. I got the knack of being friendly with the right kids. The ones who would look after me. School didn't work. Mum told me it was my only chance to get on, but I didn't listen. I thought I knew best. I thought I was tough. I kept getting excluded from classes and skiving off.

"You didn't know your father?"

"Naah. Mum said he was a salesman – vacuum cleaners. It was only when I met Paul, the guy who manages the shelter, that I started to read books and improve my writing. I read them and we talk about them. Occasionally I write a note for Paul, telling him what a particular book is about. Paul corrects the notes in red ink like a schoolteacher. Not bad, eh? Got my own tutor.

"Money was always short in our house. Mum liked a drink. And cards. And bingo. She worked in a knitting factory along Manciple Street when she was well enough. Hell, when I was about eight, I used to go down the market and pinch fruit and vegetables and the odd bit of meat or fish. Got picked up by the fuzz a few times. Told'm the truth. Told'm Mum and I were hungry. Got sent to Social Services."

"You've never been to court?" Josie asked.

"Never, touch wood. Been picked up by the cops a few times. You?"

"Twice. Possessing cocaine. I was selling on the side both times but the lawyers squashed that. Big spiel by them. Fines and probation."

Jimmy felt his record was a little dull. "I only lifted food. I got used to workin' little jobs. Delivering newspapers and parcels. Sweeping up. Stacking in a factory. The bigger I got, the better the jobs. Shiftin' furniture. A bit of cleanin' offices. You can always pocket a few things on these cleanin' jobs: biscuits, whisky, towels, cleanin' stuff, you know. No questions asked. That's how we lived until Mum died. I was about thirteen. She was a smoker. Cancer. I went into a Social Services home. Betty Thrussell in the next-door flat took me out. She was a great pal of my mother's. I eventually began earnin' enough to make it worthwhile for Betty. When I was eighteen I got a job as a cleaner at St Edith's and you know the rest."

"You've had a hard time, Jimmy."

"No I haven't!" he said exuberantly. "I've had a good time. Learned a lot. Butchers' Row was an OK place."

He understood that Josie had never focused on a person with a background like his; it was not repulsive to her, but slightly unacceptable, lower-class, despite having herself touched the lowest, lower than he could ever allow himself to go. He had no moral criticism of her, no concern that she had had many men, only an inability to grasp how she could sell herself. It was the same impulse, an inability to indulge, that held him out of the gutter of alcohol, drugs, soup kitchens and doss houses. He sensed a kind of balance between them; she uncomfortable with his beginnings; he disconcerted by the depths she had plumbed.

"Where are you going, Jimmy?" she asked.

"The big life-plan question?" He tucked his hands behind his head and stared up at the watermarks on the ceiling. "Away from this place."

"Where?"

"I dunno," he said, because it seemed over-ambitious to say that he had secretly thought of Australia. "Some place where the sun shines and I can get comfortable with a girl and maybe even have a family."

"What will you do, I mean…"

"For a livin'? Have my own business."

"What sort?"

"Any sort. I'm not much good to anybody else except as a fetch and carry man. I ain't doin' slavin'. Not *all* my life. I'm doin' that now. Stowing the dosh away. When I have enough, I'll be done with it."

"Uh-huh," Josie said, sounding unconvinced.

"Y'see this is why I have to have my own business. Might be makin' pies. Might be rentin' bikes. I dunno."

"Oh, Jimmy, you are sweet," Josie said, leaning over him and kissing him on the lips.

He could feel it was a kiss of kindness, tinged with pity. She didn't understand how strong his resolution was or how confident he was of achieving his goals.

13

When Jimmy reported to Toby with his collecting cans he found him alone. After the accounting, he said, "You didn't tell me about Rita Durbin."

"I was not seeking to hide anything from you my friend. I just forgot to mention her."

"We've got to watch out for each other, Toby. This guy Hamish is a lot smarter than Sneed. He knows drugs were used at the party."

"I would be surprised if my gentlemen indulged."

"Oh balls! You were with me. I saw it. You saw it. Did you supply?"

"Never. Not me, my boy. My commercial interests do not extend to the nefarious."

"Kevin Thrussell?"

"There is a high probability."

"And he moved the body?"

"If the body was moved, it's possible. But I beg you, my son, not to get into the detail of this unfortunate event."

Jimmy had got used to interpreting what Toby said, rather than accepting it at face value. He decoded Toby's evasiveness as confirmation of what he had guessed himself: that Kevin was involved with the arrangements for the party, supplied the drugs and removed the body.

"I want to see which way things are goin', Toby. I don't want to get screwed up by a pack of liars."

"A sentiment I share with you."

"There's one more thing about the party, Toby. Garnet was apparently wearing a camera."

Toby instantly looked sick. "Oh, no! We've got enough trouble already. What exactly has that little angel done?"

"Filmed the whole thing, she says."

"Jeez." Toby deflated over the table-top. His head and thick neck retracted into his shoulders. "What'd she get on camera?"

"Fuckin' and perving she said."

"Never. Couldn't have happened."

"She's goin' to cop a bundle selling it to the papers."

Toby considered this with narrowed eyes for a moment and then began to draw his bulk up. His glance brightened as he reflected and he exuded a huge breath. "Garnet the businesswoman. But there could be a better deal on offer, Jimmy. Don't you see? Why not?"

"Blackmail."

"Catesby? Oh no, I would never engage in such a thing. Catesby makes a bid, offers a price to save his reputation, his glorious career, almost his life, because the great Catesby with his gorgeous plumage couldn't live in prison."

"Don't have anything to do with it, Toby. The party was a murder scene."

"We have to calculate the risks. There's big, really big money here..." Toby said, smiling to himself now and ruminating as his eyes searched the dusty window frame with its broken venetian blind hanging at an angle. "You want in on it?"

"No way." Jimmy appreciated the incongruity of sitting in this decrepit room and contemplating a fortune, so much so that it seemed to him to be a fantasy.

"You want to see the film, my lad?"

"Yeah. I want to know," Jimmy said emphatically. He was

embroiled in this web and it was instinctive that knowing what happened would enable him to better protect himself. There was only a small, weak part of him that wanted to close his eyes and block his ears to everything connected with Eva.

"That dear, sweet creature, Garnet, will surely not have captured the most exquisite moments, but we must see." Toby was ecstatic.

"Ah, my little sugar, so nice to take morning tea with you," Toby said to Garnet Peabody as she came into his room with Jimmy.

Garnet was stocky, young, and moved with athletic fitness. Her hair was a mass of dark, small curls around succulent purple lips. "Jimmy says you've got some ideas about the video. Roland and me are fussed a bit by this murder stuff." She sat down in front of Toby's desk and opened her eyes expectantly.

"Well you may be, Garnet-girl. Fussed, confused, somewhat in a dither. What do your pretty pictures say?"

She thought for a moment. "They make it look bad for Catesby, Toby."

"Indeed? I'm sure Mr Catesby is a man of impeccably moral behaviour."

She sniggered. "He's a sexo and you know it."

"I have no knowledge of what may be in the great man's underpants – unless you invite me to the premiere of your work."

"I'll give you a disc. You can play it yourself. I don't want to watch it again. But what can you do, Toby?"

"I can act as your agent in selling your work to one of the tabloids which guard our decent behaviour every day. I will use my not inconsiderable negotiating skills to get you the best price, subject to my own well-earned fee of twenty-percent. You will have a goodly sum more than you could get by your own efforts. Hackville is a jungle. A darling like you shouldn't go there."

"Yeah. We was even thinkin' of putting the disc in the post anonymous to the *Sun* or the *Mail.*"

"Do not think of putting this object of your undoubted skill in a wastebasket when it can be transmuted into pure gold. I will be the alchemist."

"OK, Toby. I'll bring the disc in." Garnet began to rise from her chair.

"A moment, sweet maiden. I have yet a further proposition for you."

"You're not seriously going to do this, are you?" Jimmy asked.

"What's up?" Garnet said, subsiding.

Toby held his palms up in benediction. "Peace, children. Let us be very clear, as the politicians say when they are being obscure. Transparency between us. Yes. We should discuss this."

"What are you getting at, Toby?" Garnet said.

"My dearest girl, there is another option, not merely gold plated, but solid 22 carat."

"It's dangerous, Toby," Jimmy said.

"I am valiant in the face of danger, a warrior!"

"And it's criminal."

"That's a point of law. And for every lawyer with that point, there's another with a different point."

Jimmy shook his head negatively. Garnet looked from one to the other in consternation.

"Consider this, my two good friends. I say to Milord Catesby that there is a certain video of his cavorting. He says, from the depths of his heart, as well as his pocket, that he would like to acquire it for a certain sum. I respond by proposing my humble self as his agent to affect his wishes. Where's the crime in that?"

"You're arsing about, Toby. It's blackmail," Jimmy said.

"I don't want to do anything illegal," Garnet said. "Roland's probably going to be picked for the British squad for the Rio Games and we're getting married."

"I will protect you, dear lady. I will place a firewall of silence between you and this transaction."

"Suppose Catesby won't play?" Garnet said.

"He has to. Or see an end to his angelic reputation and probably his liberty. Don't you see there's a huge guarantee of privacy in this option?"

Garnet looked at him shrewdly. "What are you thinking of in money terms, Toby?"

"Ten or twenty thousand from a newspaper. Maybe a quarter of a million from the Catesby vault. It depends on the video, as yet unseen."

Jimmy was silent. He thought Garnet had a calculating look. "I'll talk to Roland," she said.

Garnet Peabody was persuaded by Toby to let him see the film and adopt the 22 carat option.

The viewing took place in Toby's office after the homeless had been put to bed. The two men sat before a small screen in the dark and Toby inserted the disc. The private dining room of the Dog & Duck came up on the screen in colour.

"My dear James, we have here the open door of an exclusive gathering… but the lovely Garnet has obviously saved her fire until the proceedings were well under way."

The first shots showed the tables laden with used plates, bottles and glasses. The guests, easily identifiable, were the Ravens, strewn on the surrounding couches in various stages of undress and presumably sobriety. Quick, but recognizable, shots of Gloria Thrussell and Eva Walecka appeared. Sloan seemed to be asleep. One sequence showed Hassett snorting a line of coke, another had Gloria Thrussell jigging on Montfort's lap, facing him, her dress spreading over his lower parts. There were pills scattered on a table with a hypodermic needle, a glass, a bottle of water and a tube of K-Y Jelly.

Catesby was not to be seen, but shortly Garnet's lurching camera found him in shirtsleeves and red boxer shorts. He seemed to come forward and grab her and the screen went dark. Then there was a scene of Rita Durbin in black tights beating Sloan's bare arse with a cane, his shorts around his knees, with a drooling audience of Cutforth and Montfort. The last shot showed Catesby lurching out of one of the side rooms unsteadily, with his striped shirt on and his tie hanging loosely, naked below now except for his red socks, his penis limp. The camera stole a look past him, to the couch and the inert body of a girl, with her silver dress pulled up to her waist, otherwise unclothed, face down, with her legs strewn about as though broken. The screen went black.

Toby switched the light on but it made little impression on the darkness. Both men were quiet.

"You've just watched a murder, Toby."

"Not necessarily, my friend, not necessarily, although I must admit that the noble Catesby might not fare well before a jury with that last shot. I don't think sweet Garnet's thought too much about what she's got here."

Toby switched on the screen and they watched the last few seconds again. The door opened suddenly and Kate Martin put her head in. "Sorry," she said. "I'll leave these files for you, Toby." She put the files on the nearest shelf and shut the door.

"You don't want to tell Kate?" Jimmy asked.

"I don't think Kate's liberal views, flexible and generous as they are, would extend to trading the film with Catesby."

"Don't do it, Toby. It's interferin' with justice or summit like that. Y' could get ten years."

14

When Jimmy had finished his day's work he and Josie retired to his room. They drank whisky and made love and then talked. She told him about her exotic holidays abroad. And a little about her life before the clinic. They discussed the films they had seen together and the characters in the community around Butchers' Row, inevitably coming to the fate of the Night Shelter, Eva and the police investigation.

"You're not worried are you, Jimmy?"

"Why should I be?" he said indignantly. "I ain't done nothin'."

He hadn't mentioned Garnet's video to Josie. This had convinced him that Catesby was the culprit, but he was curious about Catesby's predilections. He felt that there was a sexual angle to Josie's complaints. "You gonna tell me about Catesby?" Jimmy asked.

"Sure… it's hate I suppose. He's a louse and I could kill him without a qualm."

"Hey, that's heavy."

"Nobody you want to kill, Jimmy?"

"Naah."

"It's maybe the usual stepdaughter thing. You already know it's much worse than that. Oh yes, he tried to screw me a couple of times. Easy meat coming out of the shower, you know. I was sixteen. I felt he was hunting me, waiting for an opportunity to pounce. Maybe this is a happening with all sixteen-year-old stepdaughters.

"I stepped out of the shower one day and the bathroom door opened. This was *my* bathroom, en-suite with my bedroom. Catesby came in I remember in a powder blue towelling robe over his pot belly. He had thin, nauseating brown legs. I was uneasy with him, but I hadn't thought it necessary to lock the bedroom door in my own home. He'd groped me a few times before and I knew it wasn't parental affection. I didn't like him. I didn't trust him sexually. Maybe there are a lot of stepdaughters like that, but they get by. Nothing happens. This time something did happen.

"'My dear,' he said, he grinned lecherously and looked straight at my nakedness.

"'Get out!' I shouted.

"He came toward me and took me by the shoulders. 'There's no need to be like that, my dear. Let's be friends,' he said.

"I tore away and stepped back into the shower cubicle, slamming the door. 'If you don't get out of here this instant, I'll start screaming.'

"'Oh, that would be really silly. You'll upset the household.' Actually, there was nobody else in the house but the pair of us.

"'It should be upset!'

"'Nobody will hear you. Your mother's gone out, anyway. Come on, Martine. Be nice.'

"Grinning stupidly, he pulled the shower door open and stood staring at me. I made no particular gesture to cover myself; I was too angry. He let his robe fall open and took his erect prick in his hand.

"I just couldn't get it into my head how this unattractive, three times my age man could have the nerve or the conceit or be so narcissistic to think that *he* was desirable to a sixteen-year-old girl. But it came to me in a second that he could only be unbalanced and that was the really terrifying realization. There wasn't the slightest element of the consensual. 'Be nice' was an impossible, meaningless and irrelevant phrase. This was where I was to be the victim of his lust. And part of the realization was that maybe, in his craziness, resistance was 'being nice'.

"'Don't you understand?' I said, 'I loathe you and find you repulsive. I'd sooner fuck with a dog than you!'

"'Some dogs might be quite good.' He leered at me.

"'I've warned you!' I said. And I said it in bloody near a scream.

"'I can do you a lot of good, so you better be nice to me,' he said. He reached a hand toward my breasts. I could see flames in his eyes. He didn't seem to care what I said. He wasn't hearing me. He was relishing this. He was excited by my resistance. He actually *wanted* a physical fight. He grabbed me by the throat and began to squeeze. Not just a hand-hold. He began to throttle me, dug his fingers in. And he had the most terrifying expression. A kind of mad grin. I couldn't breathe. I could feel myself weaken. I thought I was going to faint.

"He was standing on the tile floor perhaps three inches lower than the cubicle. I thought I was gone, but I lashed out with my foot, luckily hitting him in the balls. He leaped back with a yelp and crumpled up.

"He couldn't do anything except swear at me: 'Fucking bitch!'

"In a second I was past him and through the door into my bedroom and then out of the bedroom door into the hall.

"I turned for a moment and shouted, 'Get out of my room! I'll be in the lounge, waiting for you.'

"I pulled a top-coat out of the closet in the hall, put it on and went through to the lounge and sat down. In the silence, I seemed to collapse inside. A few minutes later he came in, hastily dressed in trousers and a sweater, with bare feet.

"'This is quite ridiculous…' he began.

"He had changed his personality again. He had reverted to the oily Catesby, from the crazy man I saw in the bathroom.

"But the sight of him was enough to re-charge me. 'Get this into your head, Arnold. Unless I have an absolute assurance from you now – I mean *now* – that nothing like this will ever happen again, I'll talk to Mom, to everybody.'

"He looked at me icily, weighing what was to be gained or lost. 'I'm a very tolerant person. You should play along with me. I can make or break your life.'

"'I meant what I said about loathing you.'

"'Your mother will think you're just stirring the shit. She won't believe you.'

"'I don't care. I will talk. I'll shout!'

"'You're an unbalanced tear-away.'

"'Do I get the promise?'

"A long pause followed while Catesby calculated. He wasn't used to being given an ultimatum. I remember the noise of a motor-mower from outside entered the room, a sound which suggested that it was peaceful and sunny out there. Then the lock of the front door clicked.

"'OK,' Catesby said quickly.

"My Mom, Carol, came into the room. She must have seen an unusually dressed family with drawn faces. 'What's the matter?'

"'Nothing!' Catesby snapped, heading to leave the room.

"'He just tried to rape me, Mom.' I couldn't help letting it out I was so overwrought. 'Look at this!' and I pointed to the red marks on my throat.

"Catesby looked horror-struck and in his look, you know, there was malevolence there for me. 'Lying bitch! It's just the reverse!'

"Mom walked out of the room without a word or a sign and I had made an enemy of Catesby. He couldn't understand why I didn't keep quiet, since he'd said what I wanted. I just thought he was a deranged and unscrupulous bastard and Mom came into the room… and I blew it."

"Did your mother believe you?"

"I don't know. I think she did. But it's difficult for a woman in that position – in between. I know she was deeply involved with Catesby. He is kinda like a Svengali. I don't think she was physically afraid of him as I was, but he was violent with her at times. I saw the marks. She never complained. I never asked. Perhaps she regarded him as a raging bull. And ever since she married him there was a rift between us. Not something you talk about openly. A feeling on my part that she had betrayed my father and a feeling of guilt on hers."

"So you were you scared of him?"

"Yeah. I didn't trust him. I felt he meant to get me. I took care not be alone with him. I mean, very alone."

15

Jimmy saw Kevin alone in Harry's Cafe at lunchtime on Saturday. He bought a sandwich and a cup of coffee and went over to the short, freckled, ginger-haired youth, thickset and sturdy under a layer of fat. "Mind if I siddown?"

"Suit yourself," Kevin said, head down over fish and chips.

"You ain't doin' any further education now?"

"Don't be funny. Not at school anyhow," Kevin laughed, grimly.

Kevin, like Jimmy, had spent most of his later school career dodging or being excluded from school.

"With the Butcher Boys then?" Jimmy said, low-key.

"Mind your fuckin, biz," Kevin said, squirting tomato sauce on to a slab of white bread, folding the bread and stuffing it into his mouth. A line of red sauce ran down his chin.

"Pity about Eva."

Kevin jerked and looked squarely at Jimmy for the first time with his pale blue eyes. "Yeah, pity."

"Y'know what 'appened?"

"How would I know?" he barked, licking his greasy fingers.

"The body was in your place."

"Ma's shack? It never was there. Ma says so. So get your ideas sorted."

"Betty showed me Eva's body inside the front door of your place."

"No, no way. Ma told the cops the truth."

Jimmy had resigned himself to Betty Thrussell saying whatever would protect her son. "There was a party, wasn't there, across at the Dog? You in on that?"

"You a cop's nark or somethin'?"

"The cops will be on you if you touched the body."

"Don't I know it? Lissen, I got nothin' to worry me."

"Smooth."

Kevin pushed his plate away with satisfaction. "You expect me to be like you? Cleanin' bogs at St Edith's? You're a big success, you are. I want some things, mate. Like this." He held up his arm with a gold chain on his wrist.

Kevin was certainly dealing – that was the word in their manor and Jimmy thought he might have been using. "It's an OK job at St Edith's," he said, quietly.

"Naaaah! Now here's an offer for you." Kevin curled his lips and brayed with the confidence of a thirty-year-old. "You join us and we'll look after you. Better than lying on your bed readin' porn and wankin'."

"I don't like bein' pushed around," Jimmy said. "Not by anybody. Sure not by crazies."

"Careful, man, careful. Don't diss me. Nobody's pushed around. Respect. That's what we have. Respect for each other."

"You think the gang's decisions are your own. You think you got power."

"I got power." Kevin grinned arrogantly.

"You're talkin' a language I don't understand."

"Then you're the one that needs to go back to school!"

Jimmy had had a lot of pressure to join the Butcher Boys from Kevin's associates. He had never responded. He was wary of them. He saw them collectively as being like stormy weather, unpredictable in their violence; and like the weather, mindless, moving according to a code of what they called respect, unleashing pain on others that somehow neutralised the suffering of their own lives. Although Jimmy had to admit that the Butcher Boys, with their drug dealing and burglaries, usually had plenty of bread.

"You makin' it nicely with the dealin'?" Jimmy asked as he rose from the table.

"I ain't a fuckin' parson and the money is good."

Jimmy went back to St Edith's and told Toby about the meeting. "Kevin Thrussell has turned up and he's pretty easy."

Toby said, "He's getting a good apprenticeship. And talking of Kevin, I had Madame Durbin in this morning throwing a little more sand into the gears."

"We know about her work, Toby. What's up?"

"I said to her, 'What ails thee fair maid?'

"'Don't give me that shit, Toby,' she says, 'I didn't want to talk on the phone because I don't trust nobody.'

"'Unburden yourself, my love. These walls keep their secrets,' says I, a little deflated and prepared for bad news.

"'Yeah. That's what it's about, secrets,' she says.

"'We should have none between us, dear Rita.'

"'No, well we won't. I want five hundred quid.'

"'But, my darling, you've been paid,' I insist. 'And generously. A deal is a deal. I can't go back to my gentlemen at this late time and ask for more.'

"'This is something else. Unforeseen.' And she mentions the mystery name, Kevin Thrussell.

"I paused, carefully, smelling the air. 'Ah, the worthy Kevin,' I say.

"'He was promised for doing a job,' she says.

"'Rearranging Eva's resting place?' I try on, tentatively.

"'Yeah.'

"'But he's made a fine cock-up of it.' I try to dismiss the idea. I don't want to go back to King Catesby with it. It's above my pay grade.

"Madame launches in with passion. 'Never mind that,' she says, 'We all have a stake in this. Your gentlemen, as you call them, the fucking animals. I have a nice business, Toby, and I don't want it shut down by a murder enquiry. It was in all our interests that the body was removed.'

"'Had it been done with due finesse. I'm speaking my dear lady as one who was not a party to the arrangement.'

"'I don't give a monkey's,' Madame says. 'The dough has to be paid to keep that hardball quiet.'

"'Rumour has it that Kevin gets most favoured nation treatment from you, dear lady. Surely you can persuade him of the unwisdom of pressing his claim.'

"'Kevin wants his dough.'

"'He's sitting on the edge of a volcano himself, supplying at a murder scene. It was a murder, wasn't it?'

"'I'll tell all if I'm charged with anything,' she says. 'Meantime, Toby, the fuse on the dynamite is lit and we could all be blown apart, including *you*!'

"I capitulate. 'OK, fair lady. I will consult the paymaster.'"

"So, she didn't deny Kevin was supplying," Jimmy said.

"I would have said that the young man is in this up to the gold chain round his throat."

"Why did he screw up with the body?" Jimmy said, trying to understand. "I mean he got it across the road and dropped it finally a few yards down the corridor. I saw him when I was coming away from Betty's, comin' in the flats with a black bin bag. I thought he had other ideas than Tomachek's doorway."

"I would speculate, from what you say, that Kevin rested Eva's remains at the flat temporarily, believing his mother was out for a time. He went out himself to get vestments for the funeral. Goodness knows what was in his muddy mind in the way of a final resting place. Madam Thrussell comes home unexpectedly. Sees poor Eva and her incisive mind registers that the precious Kevin must be involved. Where is he? Panic. Calls her white knight, James Morton. Move the body! James, alas, refuses. And Kevin, returning home, finds his dear parent in a froth and realising you have seen the body, he panics too. His subtle and daring plan collapses. Suffering from poverty of imagination, he dumps Eva on Johan."

"Yeah, I guess that could be right. After we met that night, Kevin coulda freaked out," Jimmy mused. "Sounds very possible."

16

After working as Jimmy's begging partner for several weeks, Josie became depressed. She explained to him that she felt isolated, almost as alone except for him and the dog as she had been in the clinic. "I'm wanted by the police and I could be sent back to the secure clinic."

Jimmy knew about the pains of a recovering junkie. "Maybe Catesby could be persuaded to call off the bulls," he suggested.

"How could I talk to him? He'd bundle me back to the lock-up. I'm clean now and I need to talk to him."

"Whyn't call him?"

"He has dicks working for him. He'd track the call. I'm not sure I could handle it."

"You got a friend who could do it? Get Catesby to promise he'd sort the cops. He could do it like snapping his fingers. If there was a few quid for the guy you clocked, what's that to him?"

"I don't think anybody I know, anybody I could ask, would trust me or they'd say I was sick. Catesby would find me. There's only you, Jimmy and at least you know Catesby."

"Sure, he's my new best pal… I already told you I don't know him at all. He's a guy who sits opposite me at a table every few weeks for about two hours. He notices me like he notices a scratch on the table."

He saw that he had been unintentionally talking himself

into a task he didn't relish. He felt sympathetic toward Josie and a degree of animosity toward Catesby. At one time he would have been diffident about approaching Catesby, even nervous. But after he had seen and thought about the film, the patina on Catesby's shining personality had faded. Catesby had become a strange predatory animal to him, a human-sized beetle with hypnotic eyes. He had no wish to deal with the man, but he had no qualms about talking to him now. One of his rules was to draw a clear line around other people's business and not intrude, but he reluctantly agreed to be the intermediary.

Jimmy waited for Catesby in the hall at St Edith's before a board meeting and asked if he could have a private word with him afterwards. Catesby paused, showing astonishment. "What is it?" he said, brusquely.

"Can we speak after? It'll only take a few minutes."

Catesby looked puzzled as he glanced at this watch. "I have to get away sharply afterwards, but yes, a couple of minutes." He bustled away. Jimmy appreciated that Catesby was too shrewd to avoid what might be useful and too cynical of humankind not to understand that even the Jimmy Mortons sometimes knew something useful.

After the board meeting, Catesby let other members get away before him. There was therefore no embarrassment in being waved in to a small side-room by Jimmy. It was damp and cold. The electric light was dim. The Formica surface of the table between them was smeared with crumbs and jam from a staff lunch. Catesby moved reluctantly as though any private issue with Jimmy was distasteful and he was expecting to be importuned.

"Filthy place," he said. "Now, Morton, be quick."

"Martine Cleland," Jimmy said.

Catesby's eyes swelled with rapt attention. "My stepdaughter. You know where she is? Where is she?" Catesby subsided into his seat, a pretended ease.

"She's well. She wants to meet you. She wants you to get the police off her back first."

Catesby coloured slightly. "Now wait a minute, Morton. I want to know where Martine is."

"I can't tell you that. I'm not sure where. I can only tell you she wants to talk. She's had a detox and she's well."

"She's a very sick, unbalanced girl. She needs medical help, and if you don't tell me where she is, I'll call the police and hand you over…"

Jimmy had anticipated this reaction and thought it out. "It won't do any good. I don't know where she is. I don't even have a telephone number. I'm tellin' you and I'll tell the police if necessary. I had a call from her. She wouldn't tell me her address." Jimmy felt he was taking a risk here; obstructing the police was serious. He had to hope that the lure of a meeting would make Catesby more conciliatory. "Martine wants a deal with you about the property."

"What property, Morton?"

"I have no idea. I'm tellin' you what she told me. Just that." Jimmy was trying hard to edit himself out of the exchange.

Catesby was quiet for a moment. "All right. She knows where my office is…"

"No, she said she'd let me know where to meet and I'll tell you. She also wants a letter about the police, first."

Catesby jerked back in his chair, affronted. "What do you mean?"

"Call 'em off."

"The impudence!"

Jimmy waited.

Catesby brooded. "Very well. Let me know. I'll give you a letter for her. What are you to her, Morton?"

"Nothin'. You know me. I work at the shelter. She was there. Not now. She called me outta the blue."

Catesby grunted suspiciously. He removed an embossed card from his wallet. He dropped it on the table, flicking it toward Jimmy; it stuck in the jam. "Call me at that number." He stood up, picked up his briefcase and left the room without a further word.

In spite of his rudeness, Catesby complied in a few days. Jimmy passed a letter to Josie informing her that the police had assured Catesby that they had completed their investigation. The complainant had agreed to withdraw the charge of assault. The file would be closed and there would be no police proceedings. "It doesn't say that Catesby arranged to pay off the guy but that's what must have happened," Jimmy said.

Jimmy and Josie agreed the letter cleared the way for Martine to make a personal appearance and he arranged another meeting with Catesby. It took place in one of the empty offices on the first floor after a board meeting. The room was cold and ill-lit. Josie was standing by the window wrapped in a coat and scarf looking out into the darkness. She turned when they came in.

"Martine, my dear!" Catesby went forward but she dodged behind the table.

"Let's stick to business, Arnold."

Catesby looked at Jimmy. "We don't need you any more, Morton."

"Yes, we do. Jimmy must stay."

"But Martine, we're going to discuss family business…"

"Jimmy stays. I don't trust you, Arnold."

Catesby puffed air from his tight lips. "That's very-"

"That's the way it is. Sit down, Jimmy," Martine said.

She seemed to have no difficulty now in facing Catesby calmly. Jimmy sat down; the awesome Catesby had become, for him, a dangerously unstable person, yet he looked so placid in his elegant suit, the genial businessman. Jimmy was on edge as he watched Catesby preparing to ease his way around Josie, to renew his hold on the person who controlled the land that was key to his project.

Catesby breathed heavily and shook his head as though these proceedings were quite unjustified; the venue, Morton's presence, Martine's remarks, everything. Then he said, in soft and fatherly tones, "You're pale and thin…"

"Don't worry about my health. Let's talk about the estate."

"You're still taking drugs," he scoffed, his mood changed.

"Not since I left your goddamn clinic. I'm clean. That's why I'm here. I know your plans for this place, Arnold. I know you're putting up a plan covering the estate land *which you don't own or control.* I want to know how you're going to deal the estate in."

"I don't know where you get your information from, my dear. Morton perhaps? Divulging confidential matters. It's cockeyed. Nothing of the sort, Martine." Catesby had an amused note which clashed with his bleak stare.

"I ain't talked to Martine about board business," Jimmy interrupted, "not once. Not on any subject." In fact, Josie hadn't even discussed with him what she was going to say at the meeting.

"You keep quiet, Morton," Catesby said.

"Arnold, it's common knowledge around the shelter that it's smack in the middle of a big redevelopment proposal.

By you. But the land as well as the St Edith's buildings belong to the Cleland estate."

"My dear girl, you don't know anything about this area…"

"When I was sixteen, Dad brought me down here. He wanted to show me the shelter and the other things St Edith's was doing. He told me he was on the board. He explained that the shelter was part of a valuable block of land. His land. He said it needed redevelopment and maybe I'd have something to do with that when I grew up. I know what I'm talking about."

This was news to Jimmy.

"You've got it wrong." Catesby waved a white hand and stood up. "Let me have your address for future reference."

"Speak to Jimmy if you want to make a deal. He'll set up a meeting."

Catesby's face tightened and without glancing at Jimmy he hustled out of the door.

"Not good, eh?" Jimmy said.

Josie's face cracked into a grin for the first time that evening. "Oh, yes. That asswipe has the message. He'll think about it. He'll come back. As long as I'm clean, he has to."

17

Hamish liked the police practice of making early morning calls – catching the witness or criminal unawares. He liked to see them groping for meaning. He didn't make appointments with suspects in murder cases, except of course people like the directors of St Edith's. There was a certain kind of person who would complain bitterly to his superiors if he dug them out of bed too early in the day or cluttered the street with police cars in a dawn raid. Rita Durbin was not that kind of person. She was next on his list. She lived in quite a tall stylish block of private apartments in Curfew Street which was only a few blocks away from the squalor of Butchers' Row.

He was accompanied by two detective sergeants from the murder squad. They forced the street door of the building quickly, climbed the stairs to Durbin's fourth floor rooms and rang the bell. She came to the door, opened it a crack on a chain and twisted her head round the edge. Her hair was under a net and her face oily.

"Police, Ms Durbin. About the murder of Eva Walecka." Hamish smiled. "Can we come in?"

"No, you can't."

"Take a look at this," Hamish said, proffering a piece of paper through the crack in the doorway.

Durbin squinted at the document. "A warrant?"

"Yes. Shouldn't be necessary to attack your door."

"OK" she said, mournfully, letting the door open. They

followed her down the hall and into a dark and curtained lounge. Durbin drew the drapes open. The floral carpet clashed with the embossed paper on the walls. Two quite exact oils of landscapes hung above the couches. Not cheap, Hamish thought. Whisky and vodka bottles were standing on a cabinet, with a collection of used glasses.

They all sat down at Durbin's invitation. She seemed resigned, huddling in a fluffy pink dressing gown. Hamish took out his small recorder and switched it on. He was aware that Durbin was a self-employed sex worker and a shop steward in a union which looked after the interests of sex workers.

"I'll ask my colleagues to have a look round while we talk. I hope you'll be prepared to help us." He gave her a formal warning about her rights which she shrugged off.

"I've got nothing to hide. Go ahead."

"About the party at the Dog & Duck. You've said to Mr Sneed that you didn't see anything untoward. No drug taking?"

"I didn't see any."

"Did you see or hear any of the girls suffering physical abuse?"

"Nothing. No."

"Do you know Mr Catesby?"

"I know who he is. You wouldn't expect him to be a friend, would you?"

"Seen him before?"

She hesitated. "Yes."

"How long ago?"

She waved her hands in a confused way. "I don't know. Six months."

"He's a client?"

"OK, he's a client."

"What does he like?"

"Look, that's private. I have a business and..."

"This is a murder enquiry, Ms Durbin, which rests on sexual violence. You work in the field of sexual violence yourself. You have worked with this man. Now tell me about him."

There was a long pause. "Nothing. Catesby's all right. He's always treated me well. He's... whipping and dressing up..."

"You've had sex with him. Has he ever attacked you?"

"Only, like playing, play acting."

"Pretend rape?"

"Yeah, I guess."

"Does he pretend to choke you as part of it?"

"Only pretending. It's all pretending. Look, I'm not saying any more and I don't see..."

"Let's leave it there. Did you work with any of the other men or women who were there that night?"

"Yes. Mr Hassett and Mr Montfort."

"Are any of them people you've worked with on another occasion?"

"No. I don't think I can help you any more. I want a cup of coffee."

"Did you know the murdered girl?"

Durbin's interest sparked. "I had spoken to her in the past, poor thing."

"What about?"

"About getting the fuck out of the hands of her pimp."

"Did you talk to her at the party?"

"No."

"The other girls there were Garnet Peabody and Gloria Thrussell, you know them?"

"By sight. They live around here."

While Rita Durbin went to the kitchen, Hamish was able to speak to his men who had returned from their search. She made coffee for all of them and they sat down.

Hamish said, "We've had a look at the equipment you have here without disturbing any of it. We are going to make a forensic examination and we may want to ask you some questions about it later. By the way, do you know Kevin Thrussell, brother of Gloria?"

"Sure. He's a local kid."

"A dealer?"

"I don't know about that."

"Was he there at the pub?"

"No."

"Eva's pimp, Johan?"

"I know him by sight and by reputation. He was around the Row that night."

"So why was Eva at the party? She didn't work that way, did she?"

"She might have been moonlighting to make a bit of money of her own. God knows she wanted to get away from here. Or maybe Johan fixed up a different deal for the party. I don't know."

When the forensic team arrived, Hamish came away from the apartment. He said to his two assistants, "She told me something interesting about Catesby. I didn't think she'd go so far, but she knew what she was doing. She's as hard as flint."

Hamish thought that Rita Durbin was a canny businesswoman and she had wanted to impress him that she was also straightforward. She just wanted the police off her shoulder.

Hamish sat in Turk's small office at the Jarndyce Street station. He felt it was more of a confrontation than a meeting. Turk loomed over Hamish and Sneed from his high chair behind the desk.

Hamish wasn't very impressed after working with Ed Turk and Bill Sneed. Turk, who was a Pakistani ethnic, had a volcanic manner, simmering but capable of blowing. Sneed looked to Hamish like a sleazy pickpocket.

Hamish said, "The St Edith's board members who were at the party have clammed up on what happened. They can't deny basic facts like who was there, drug involvement and the fact that it was a fuck-fest, but it doesn't get us far enough."

"Those boys will be shakin'," Sneed said, with amusement.

"With good cause," Hamish said.

"Yeah," Turk said, "they wouldn't want *The Sun* to get hold of this."

"Any ideas? You know this lot," Hamish said.

"I wouldn't rule out the St Edith's directors, but I think they were on a frolic of their own," Turk said, cautiously.

"What we don't know is where Eva died – at Butchers' Row or the Dog & Duck? Betty Thrussell reckons her son Kevin wasn't involved. Kevin's been lying low. Not seen at any of his haunts," Sneed said.

"What's he like? A murderer?" Hamish asked with a weak smile.

"Very well could be," Sneed said. "Nasty. Dealer. Gang member. Convictions for dealing and assault. Done time in a Young Offenders'."

"Not exactly a sex maniac," Hamish said.

"We'll pick him up," Turk said.

"What about the other guy, Morton, who was called in by Mrs Thrussell? I've talked to him," Hamish said.

"Local toughie. No record. Smart. Betty Thrussell says

he moved the body. He denies it. Could be him," Sneed said.

"Friabin. I've seen him," Hamish said. "He denies he was at the party. Says he set it up. A regular date about twice a year. Claims he cleaned up afterwards with Morton's help. Evasive about the clean-up. No need to clean up according to the publican. His staff would have done it the next morning as routine. Why were they cleaning up at midnight? Merely to cover the drugs?"

"Toby Friabin's a local man. An official at St Edith's. No trouble with the law," Sneed said, softly dismissive.

"What about the pimp?" Hamish said.

"Johan Tomachek. Out of the country briefly and he says he can prove it. He's back now," Sneed said.

"We'll pick him up too," Turk said, "and give him a shake."

"The girls. What do they say? You tell me. I've talked to them," Hamish said.

Sneed said, "Garnet Peabody. Works at St Edith's. Decent family. Does a bit of pole dancing. She says that she left the pub early. Says it was supposed to be stripping not whoring."

"With couches and rugs in the back rooms?" Hamish said.

"Yeah, I know," Sneed said, "but she says she never went there. Identifies Eva as present."

"Why'd she leave early?"

"Job done," Sneed said.

"And the Thrussell bitch," Turk said. "We had her in here. Admits she was lap-dancing. Confirms Eva was there. Says she doesn't know anything."

"And Durbin?" Hamish said.

"Durbin's playin' the same tune," Sneed said. "She was there. There were three rooms. Never saw anything. She's about thirty-five. No chick. A dominatrix by trade."

"Forensics?" Turk said to Hamish.

"The rooms are constantly used for dining and parties but there were plenty of fresh prints on the furniture," Hamish said. "Threads from Eva's dress on a couch in one of the rooms. I don't think proving attendance at the party, if we have to, is going to be a problem. We have a number of different DNA specimens from Eva's body and clothes. Whoever screwed Eva that night wore a condom. We don't have any semen. We can probably match the DNA to one or more of the men who were there or perhaps Kevin Thrussell, Friabin or Morton. We'll be covering the waiters too. The match won't prove murder because she could have completed her evening's work before she got into trouble. The problem, as Bill said, is *where* Eva was murdered. And if it was at the Dog & Duck, who carried the body across the road?"

"Kevin Thrussell or Morton," Turk said.

"Or somebody else," Hamish said. "The waiters?"

"Dismissed about 9pm and the screwing hadn't started," Sneed said.

"We're not getting anywhere, are we?" Hamish said.

"We'll work on it," Turk said.

Hamish came away from the meeting thinking that there had been a slight tension. Turk and Sneed didn't strike him as a pair of honest cops pooling their knowledge of a crime. He had a feeling Turk and Sneed thought with one mind, knew more than they were telling and wanted to steer it their way. Who might they want to protect? The drift from the meeting had been Friabin, the St Edith's directors and Tomachek.

Hamish had confidentially seen the personnel files kept on Turk and Sneed through a Human Resources friend at the Yard. Both had histories checkered with a variety of complaints and disciplinary action, but they were, obviously, still officially regarded as satisfactory officers. The pair were steeped in local knowledge. Sneed had served the area for five years and Turk for two. Sneed wasn't going anywhere, but Hamish guessed that Turk was keen for promotion. Hamish juggled these thoughts inconclusively.

The crime scene was one which had facets that Hamish had seen many times before. It was clear that Eva had been murdered as part of a sex orgy. That could have been at the party, or afterwards as a one-man involvement after she crossed the road. Several identifiable people could be guilty. The St Edith's directors would surround themselves with a legal barricade. They would admit nothing, block the enquiry where they could and complain to Hamish's boss more strongly than they already had about harassment.

Hamish could smell protection too. He guessed Sneed and Turk were on the take, but from whom? Friabin? Durbin? Tomachek? Or all of them? Probably not Morton or Thrussell; they wouldn't be able to afford it. And not the directors; they had more indirect ways of protecting themselves.

Hamish considered whether he, punting quietly toward retirement, should confront these people. Should he try to smash the roadblock of evasion and solve the murder of Eva definitively? This was not a question that came to him burning for a solution. The part of him that was his heart or conscience was not involved. The question simply arose, as in the course of a journey, where he might consult a well-thumbed road map and confirm a direction that he had taken in the past.

The answer remained the same as it always had during his career: no, he wouldn't attempt to combat obstruction.

What would be the point in facing the strife he would cause to himself and his wife and family? Complaints would be made against him. He could receive a reprimand or even disciplinary action. He knew from experience that except in rare instances, the Catesbys and Hassetts and their like were near-unassailable. Something unforeseen would have to go awry in their defensive net for them to be vulnerable. Turk and Sneed, in all probability, belonged to a club which was in league with the very people he was trying to apprehend. They too would fight him by complaining about his conduct of the case if he went in any direction other than the one that they pointed to.

He hadn't quite given up solving the murder. There was a lot of routine enquiry work to be done, but he believed it wouldn't yield any clear answer about the crime. The investigation would be complete about the time he was due to retire. The file might technically remain open, but that was as far as it would go.

Hamish would admit to his wife, but only to her, that he regretted that enquiries were blocked, but he would add that corruption was like cancer, endemic in the human condition. Like cancer, it could spread to defeat the surgeon whichever organ he turned to. But there, he would say, the simile ended, because the reward for failed surgery in this case, was personal pain and possibly ruin for the surgeon.

18

Toby was enthralled with his plan to sell the film to Catesby despite Jimmy's warnings. He arranged a meeting with Garnet Peabody and her boyfriend. He enlarged upon the reward open to them that would far exceed what a tabloid newspaper would pay. "That good fortune is accessible," he said, "subject to a payment of twenty percent of that sum to my honourable self for doing the heavy lifting, so to speak."

Garnet and Roland, who were never clear how to turn their good idea into actual cash, agreed when Toby pointed out, "It can't do any harm to plumb the depths and see what fat fish we could land. Entirely my efforts. At that point you could exercise your sovereign right to choose." They had been carried along above all by anger and a desire to get even with Catesby for harassing Garnet. They had aimed to embarrass Catesby. The amount a newspaper might pay them, though welcome, was, even to them, a fantasy. But with Toby's intervention, the idea of actually extracting money from Catesby in a direct person-to-person get-even was a very attractive thought. Jimmy's warnings went unheeded; firewall or not, Garnet and Roland seemed prepared to accept that it probably wasn't blackmail at all.

Toby arranged to meet Catesby at a smart coffee shop on the South Bank one morning. He recounted the meeting to Jimmy after settling and distributing the takings for St Bernard's Dogs' Home that same afternoon. He settled in his chair with a plate of sausage rolls and glanced up to the ceiling in the manner of a man about to begin a peroration.

"This man is as discreet as a clam on a stall in the market," Toby said. "When I made the private appointment on the phone, Catesby did not question why a humble proletarian should seek an audience with a titan of finance."

"Maybe he spends a lot of time doing weird deals in the dark," Jimmy said. He never thought of Catesby without seeing the image of him lurching away from the broken body of Eva.

"Catesby was looking dapper, sitting in the best seat in the window, as you would expect, when I joined him. 'Not a very private place to chat,' I say, squeezing into one of the small chairs.

"'We're not going to chat,' he says, fiercely but quietly.

"I think I'll rile him a little, so I say, 'Something's come up.'

"'Too much has come up already, Friabin. Get it out!'

"'First, the bad news, sir.' I paused here to see whether I could inscribe a line on that fine brow, but no. 'Madame Durbin has materialized with a request for five hundred quid. She says she paid one Kevin Thrussell, a rising star hereabouts, to find a more auspicious resting place for the Polish beauty.'

"He fixed me with those eyes, like oysters on the half shell floating in tar. He spoke not at first. Then he says in that velvet voice, 'Very well. Get on with the good news.'

"What is five hundred quid to a man who deals in billions? Here, I think I might have him. 'Images,' I say, 'images.' I can see the cogs whirring around in that finely tuned mind. 'Images of *what*?' he sniffs.

"'Of your noble self, sir, and your equally splendid companions comporting yourselves in a carefree manner and wantonly displaying your physical parts.'

'''Cut the gobbledygook, man! You mean pictures taken at the public house?'

'''No, I don't.'

'''Then what the hell do you mean?'

'''I mean a film, sir, rich in detail.'

'''A film? Who was filming? Who's done this?' His voice goes up an octave here.

'''Well it wasn't me because I wasn't there for the juicy part.'

'''And it wasn't those grubby little waiters because they weren't in the room either except when summoned!' Catesby says.

'''So,' I say, 'the mantle of camera-person of the evening falls on four pure and innocent young women, one of whom has now left us.'

'''Which one had the camera?' Catesby's splendid tan has been drained like a swamp. He looks cheesy.

'''I can't tell you because I don't know.'

'''Liar!' Catesby says, not at all convinced by my seraphic visage, but he paused to suffer the impact of the news. I thought I saw a little light of desperation in his eyes.

'''You assured me the girls were… reliable. Fucking cunts!' He has stones in his mouth now when he speaks. That exquisite velvet accent has gone.

'''Precisely accurate, sir,' I reply, shocked to hear crudities soiling the lips of such a genteel gentleman.

'''How do you *know* this, Friabin?' He's rasping.

'''From a friend of a friend. Let's let the heavy burden rest there, sir.'

'''This is blackmail. How much have they asked for?'

'''Not even a copper coin. No. The direction in which this film is heading is not toward your good self or your friends, but to one of those indefatigable guardians of free speech – and viewing – who fill our news-stands and make our Sunday afternoons so interesting.'

"'A tabloid newspaper!'

"'The very same.'

"'Can this be stopped, Friabin?' he says, recovered a little, pretty calm.

"'How would you suggest, in view of a possible material motive in the camera-person?'

"'Money,' Catesby says sternly. He speaks with certitude of a man who knows that for most troubles, a monetary poultice is a more effective remedy than a dose of antibiotics.

"'Money. A fair assumption, sir. It's a bidding race. You don't have to pay anything if you don't want to.'

"'We'll pay,' he says, quickly, very quiet, hardly moving his lips as though it's indecent. 'It's a scam.'

"'No, sir. Nothing like that. I said to my informant, who had a front-page expose in mind, 'Why not give my honourable gentlemen an opportunity to purchase?' And being a reasonable person, my informant said, 'Why not?'

"Jimmy, it hadn't escaped me that Catesby had used the plural 'we' when agreeing to pay. My internal cash register logged a more healthy price as a result.

"Catesby gargled on: 'I'll need to see the film in advance and be assured that it's the only copy, *and* the only film that was taken that night.' This was the lawyer talking.

"'Of course assurances will be given,' I said, 'but this won't be due diligence as you are used to it, sir. And think of the reputations of you and your friends if you miss a chance to squash the bug at birth. You'll have to take a chance on the veracity of my informant, but there is a certainty of what will happen if you don't.'

"'Keep your speculation to yourself, Friabin. How much?'

"'Well, I should have thought that one of our finest journals would not have paid less than one hundred thousand pounds for the scalps of four such esteemed citizens and possibly two-hundred and fifty. The news will go viral as they say.'

"'We'll give you three-hundred fifty thousand. That's final.' Very quickly spoken.

"I was impressed at the speed of his rejoinder. I said, 'Sadly, no.'

"'What do you mean, man?' A tinge of alarm here, I thought.

"'I believe my reliable informant is thinking of a different range of numbers.'

"Catesby leans across to me clenching his fist on the table. I believe he would have grasped my necktie had I thought to wear one on this propitious occasion. 'You won't get as much as three fifty thousand from a newspaper! They have their limits,' he hisses.

"'Exactly the reason my informant is allowing your munificent self this option.'

"'Name it.'

"'My honourable informant is prepared to accept one million five-hundred thousand pounds, which is poker chips between you and your friends, *and* to forgo the pleasure of seeing your valorous activities blazoned across the front page of the *Mail*.'

"'Extortion!' Catesby whispers. His eyeballs enlarge, but he is still calm.

"'Let's not use harsh words. If you so instruct me I shall walk away from this café. I will even pay for our Dark Colombian. I will never mention the matter to you again and my informant will have the aforesaid pleasure.'

"I know I have him, Jim-boy. I was working a barrow

in the market when he was in prep school learning Latin. Catesby clasps his hands around the edge of the table and is silent. Head down. The great man was pondering on the edge of the abyss, so dearly does he love this petty money.

"I stood up. 'I shall have to go,' I said to him.

"'All right,' says he in a voice so low.

"'One and a half?' I confirm.

"'Arrange a viewing as soon as possible. Ring me on my mobile and keep quiet!' he spits through his teeth.

"'You can rely on me, sir. Allow me to get the check as I go out.'"

Toby had a questioning look as he finished his account. "Funny thing, Jimmy. I'd built a little come-down in my bid. One and a quarter would have been adequate and I would have reduced, but the great man had a well-concealed discombobulation and he didn't press."

A few days later Toby told Jimmy about the elaborate arrangements being made to enable the proposed payment to Garnet on Catesby's instructions. They were quite beyond Garnet and boyfriend, but Toby managed on their behalf.

"This is the way it was, Jimmy. I went to Catesby's office bearing the modest compact disc which contained that Academy Award hit, expecting a front row seat for the showing. Instead, Catesby snatched the disc from me, took it into an inner room and left me on my Pat Malone without even a cup of Earl Grey. He came back in half an hour. 'OK' says he, 'We'll buy.' He shows no embarrassment or anxiety. He could have been buying a bag of carrots.

"'A million and a half,' says I.

"'I won't suffer your dirty tricks, Friabin. I know this isn't the only disc.'

"'Upon my life, sir, it is.'

"'You'd never have handed it to me and allowed me to take it out of the room if it was, because I don't intend to hand it back…'

"Genuinely startled at this turn of events I was. 'Surely, a gentleman of your impeccable honesty…'

"'Friabin,' he trumpets, 'I want the copy you've kept. When you surrender it, you'll get your one and a half.'

"'My informant,' I say, 'will be very distressed at this reflection on his integrity, but I shall apply to him.'"

"Could be more than one disc held back," Jimmy interrupted.

"Exactly, my perspicacious young friend. The good Arnold knows that well. But he wanted to send a signal that he is up with the game. So, I went through the requested motions and produced another copy – with a suitably groveling apology."

"The maloolah was passed yesterday?"

"Into a Cayman Islands account in the name of a trustee for Garnet Peabody. But here is the clincher, Jimmy. I am in Catesby's office. Feeling isolated in that huge book-lined room with its shiny oaken desk an acre wide. Catesby rises from his chair and comes around the desk. He isn't all that tall, but he has a devilish look. He is towering over me in his fine worsted and exuding a sweet but poisonous odour. 'Friabin,' he says, 'I am going to say something which I want you to absorb in your febrile brain. If this film appears in future, you and whoever else is involved will…' and here, he paused like the great thespian he is, '*die*, Friabin. You, they, will die. Do you get that? Can you take it on board?' All this was said in calm and quiet.

"'You are threatening me, sir, an honest broker… but I understand your message and I will communicate it.'

"'Yes, I *am* threatening you, Friabin,' he says, burning me with his look."

"Howja take that, Toby?"

Toby shrugged. "Might be just a rhetorical flourish, but that man has awesome power."

19

The following afternoon, when Jimmy had finished his accounting to Toby, Garnet Peabody came into the room. She looked disheveled. She was tense.

"Hey wassa matter, baby?" Jimmy asked.

"We was robbed last night, Jimmy."

"What I hear, you can afford it," he grinned. A neighbourhood robbery was hardly news. The poor preyed on the poor regularly. Toby, too, looked complacent.

"Yeah, yeah, but you oughta see what they did! Three masked guys."

"Messed up your place?"

"Not just that. They held me and Roland down, tied us up on the floor. Gagged us. Never said a word themselves. I was shit scared. I thought I was gonna be raped. They took every digital gadget we had. TV, laptop, iPads, mobile phones and cameras and all our CDs and our computer and printer. Everything!"

"Ah, ha!" Toby exclaimed.

"Hit you?" Jimmy asked.

"Never hit Roland or me."

"So, you have no CD or copy of that delightful film you shot at the Dog & Duck?" Toby said.

"The fuckers got that too!" Garnet said.

"Never mind. You got a million and a half," Jimmy said.

"Subject to my agency fee," Toby said.

"I wouldn't have done this if I'd known…" Two big tears shone in Garnet's eyes.

"Oh, dear lady, a little discomfort for a large reward!"

"Did you report it to the police?"

"Course I bloody well didn't. We ain't got any insurance anyway."

Garnet had left the room in a huff. Toby said to Jimmy, "Milord Arnold is certainly thorough in his due diligence."

The next day, Toby received the overfull collection tins for the St Bernard's Dogs' Home glumly. His fleshy face was downcast.

"I had a rather unfortunate experience last night, Jimmy. When I arrived home at about ten o'clock, I found Amethyst being entertained by a gentleman in the lounge of our apartment. I listened from the hall. Quite eloquent he was and knowledgeable about distant places on the globe that he had visited. No, he was not a travel agent. I had him to a millimeter before I crossed the carpet to greet him. He had a shaven head, small eyes and a big chest under his t-shirt. The tattoos on his forearms were quite intricate. So *common* you might say, the pubs are full of tattooed toughies. But this man wasn't pretending to be tough. I feared, alas, he was tough.

"'How did *you* get in?' I said to him, alluding to the fact that I recognized him as vermin.

"'I was admitted lawful-like by your peachy wife, bruvver. Don't ask me more.'

"Ameythyst was sitting sedately, unharmed and all attention, knowing now, from my disturbed demeanour that all was not well.

"'Delightful place you 'ave here. Keep it nice,' he said.

"'Where you from?' I asked, trying to be friendly. He wasn't a face on our manor.

"'I'm not here for a conference, bruvver. I have a message for you.'

"'Who from?' As if I didn't know.

"'A friend in the City who shall remain nameless.'

"'I have many friends in the City, but I think I could guess,' I say.

"'We won't do quiz night at the pub, Friabin. Lissen up! If you rat on the deal with my friend, or gab to anybody about it, you will suffer a life-threatening illness.'

"'Message received and understood,' I said. 'May I show you out now?'

"'One uvver thing, mate. There is no time limit on this promise. It lasts for your lifetime like a Patty Fillip watch.'

"'You're selling a Rolls-Royce product,' I say.

"As he's going out the door he says, 'Don't get funny with me, fatso.'

"It gave me a nasty turn, Jimmy and I have given Amethyst a strict injunction to admit nobody to the Friabin castle."

"Like Garnet. More due diligence whatcha callit," Jimmy said.

"Indeed, my boy. Catesby is building walls of steel around himself and his friends, in the time honoured way of his kind."

After his meeting with Catesby and Josie, Jimmy began to remind himself of some of the arguments which he had mostly ignored at board meetings. He saw Kate and told her how Josie came to the Shelter and her connection with the Cleland Estate.

"I'm not sure where you stand, Kate. Whether you want to stop Catesby, or rely on the promise of a new buildin' elsewhere for St Edith's. But Josie – her real name is Martine Cleland – has a lot of clout over the land."

"It's very good of you to tell me this, Jimmy. I think we're going to lose whatever happens. A new building to replace the existing ones, old and decayed as they are, isn't going to be forthcoming because it would be too expensive, and when it comes it probably wouldn't be in the right place or have the space. A new St Edith's in a different place is going to be a different animal if it happens. And there's going to be a delay, could be for years. We'll all be redundant."

"So, you want to stop it?"

"I don't think it can be stopped. Unofficially, we know planning permission will be available. I can't blame the council. They'd rather have a skyscraper than a derelict homeless shelter."

"OK, so you're not mad. But suppose Josie refused to sell."

"That might hold things up for a while… the council might be able to take the land by compulsory purchase, I don't know."

"Holding up Catesby could get you better money for the shelter and the other buildings."

"Maybe. Would you like to bring her here for a talk?"

Jimmy asked Josie if she would be prepared to talk to Kate. She was living now in a run-down rental apartment, in a block not yet condemned, in Butchers' Row. She had managed to stay clear of dope and was beginning to recover a new and brighter personality which had wilted under heroin. Jimmy noted that her trust fund had apparently yielded enough for a wardrobe of presumably fashionable clothes. And she was having her hair and nails cared for professionally. She had given up begging. She and Jimmy met for the occasional meal and they sometimes slept together.

Josie listened carefully while Jimmy explained St Edith's problems, although she already understood only too well why they had come about. She asked some quite calculating questions about the buildings. "Why should I try to postpone the inevitable, Jimmy?"

"St Edith's might get a better price if you hung out."

Josie thought about this. "There's no point in me meeting Kate. I have nothing to offer her, Jimmy."

"You mean you're goin' with Catesby?"

"I made a deal with Catesby. I want the proceeds."

Jimmy heard her cool, businesslike assessment as if it was from a stranger. He didn't argue. The pretend low-lifer who had changed into the frail girl in need of protection, had now changed again into an astute woman. "OK," he said.

"Let's go and get a drink, Jimmy. I'm buying tonight. And you'll stay, won't you?"

He could feel Josie moving away from his kind of life. He could see that she was striving hard to beat the dope. She hadn't quite made up her mind to quit Butchers' Row and move back to south west London. He couldn't understand why. She still hankered after him. He was surprised at that but thought he was a convenient friend. She had no other friends he knew of and spent her time as a volunteer at the drop-in centre and at a children's nursery.

20

Hamish learned from the police handling the assault charge against Martine Cleland that it had been dropped. The complainant had declined to offer evidence. He also knew from the police file that Martine was a drug addict and the main beneficiary in the Cleland estate which owned the land on which St Edith's stood. But Hamish's interest in her was mainly as Catesby's adopted daughter. He wanted to find out about Catesby's sexual behaviour and who might know more than an adopted daughter? The fact that he thought Catesby an elusive target for a murder charge did not mean that he relented in his investigation, except of course where it might embarrass Catesby. He could only confront Catesby face-to-face when he had hard evidence that required an explanation.

One of Hamish's team found Martine's address and arranged a meeting. Hamish was let into a flat in a decrepit building in Butchers' Row by an alert, relaxed and well-groomed young woman, not the nervous ex-addict he imagined. She invited him to sit down and offered him a cup of tea which he accepted. She served them both and threw herself back on a couch in the comfortable lounge, crossing the ankles of her long legs. She wore a short dress. He glanced round the room. The walls had had a fresh coat of white paint. The curtains looked new.

"I'm afraid I'm not going to be able to help you, Inspector. I know nothing of what happened to Eva. It happened about the time I arrived here."

Hamish shrugged as though it didn't matter. They were able to talk freely for a few moments. Hamish liked to put himself in good standing with a witness before drilling down on the important questions. They talked about the changes coming to the area and the likely demise of St Edith's. He led the conversation back to the tragedy of Eva.

"There are always a lot of surrounding events that are helpful to us, Miss Cleland. For instance, you know James Morton."

"He's a friend."

"Did he tell you he'd seen Eva's body?"

"Yes. I think he was shocked. He said he was called over to his old landlady's flat. She asked him to move the body, but he wouldn't do it."

"Am I right that you used to sleep with him at Number 10 Pew Street?"

"That's my business and surely nothing to do with the case," she replied casually but firmly.

"Are you friendly with your stepfather, Mr Catesby?"

"Do we have to talk about him?"

"Yes, because on the night of Eva's death, he was with friends at a party in Butchers' Row. And we need to understand who was or might have been involved."

"Well, actually, no, we're not friends. I have a business relationship with him."

"But he is your adoptive father?"

"The reason we're not friendly is a complicated family matter and I don't want to talk about it."

Hamish was immediately sensitive to the estrangement. He presumed that Martine would be unlikely to complain or reveal his line of questioning to Catesby. "Does it have anything to do with sex?"

"That's a strange question and way off limits, surely, in your investigation."

His question had seemed to hit her. Hamish noted that her reaction wasn't the surprise or shock coupled with denial, which might have been expected. He had unearthed something. "No, it's not off limits. I'm investigating a murder by a sexual predator."

"And my stepfather is a suspect?"

"I'm not suggesting anybody in particular is a suspect. Mr Catesby was one of the people in the vicinity at the time."

"In the vicinity? You mean at the party at the Dog & Duck?"

"Yes. We have to talk to everybody, Miss Cleland. It's no use having tea with them and chatting about the weather."

"So you're talking to me and you've talked to Arnold. What does he say?"

"He doesn't want to talk to us."

He waited while she thought about this. He felt she had something she wanted to say but was trying to decide whether to say it.

"What difference could it possibly make if I said something sexually derogatory about my stepfather's behaviour? It wouldn't prove anything. It would be irrelevant."

"It would show I am probably heading in the right direction." Hamish spoke gently as though he wasn't asking for much, just a little help.

She stiffened and stared at him. After another pause, "I haven't anything to say." Her face was blank.

Hamish came away certain that there *was* something that Martine Cleland withheld, otherwise the usual reaction would have been at least a denial that there was a sexual issue, if not an endorsement of Catesby as a decent man. Martine was right: it wouldn't help in any case against Catesby, but it firmed Hamish's opinion that Catesby was likely to have predatory sexual impulses.

In Hamish's assessment, the other board members were cardboard cut-outs beside Catesby. On the surface, their backgrounds were copybook privileged middle class: public schools, top universities, faint Anglican church affiliation, marriage to equally well educated and privileged women, two or three children each, and still married to the same wife; all prosperous in their different followings. Under the surface, he expected there would be peccadilloes: carefully concealed adulteries with discreet women of their own class, experimentation with drugs, a little whoring, a small appetite for online porn, nothing very kinky. His team's research had unearthed nothing against any of these directors that would focus a murder charge.

In contrast, Catesby was a throbbing engine. When Hamish came within his aura the energy and determination the man radiated was palpable. It was easy for Hamish to believe that sexual predation was part of it.

21

They came for Jimmy at 6am. It was still dark. Just a scuffling sound outside his door which, as a light sleeper, he heard. Then the splintering crash of a boot against the flimsy door, slamming it open. And Turk rearing above him like a totem pole. Fingers plunged down to his throat, a fist tore at the t-shirt he wore.

"Get up, you little rat!"

As soon as Jimmy's feet hit the floor, Turk's open hand slapped the side of his head, knocking him back on the bed. Turk grabbed his leg and dragged him off the bed on to the floor and kicked him in the ribs. Turk put a fist under his armpit, sat him up and kicked him in the back.

"You're under arrest on suspicion of murder, you slimy little shit," Turk said.

"Right, sir, I'll take care of him," Sneed said. Jimmy pulled on a sweater and jeans under Sneed's eye and was dragged from the building by two constables. He was taken to the Jarndyce Street station. He was so confused that he hardly felt the pain of the blows. He stood shivering in a cold cell while a sergeant read him his rights. He was left alone until Hamish arrived. Hamish took him to an interview room.

"Do you want to make a statement, son? You don't have to. If you do it will be taken down and may be used against you..."

"They told me that stuff. All I wanta say is I din't have nothing to do with it! Nothin'."

"OK. You'll be taken to court this morning. You won't have to plead. You're not going to be charged. We need more time to look at your case. You'll be remanded in custody. Do you want to call a lawyer?"

"I want to call Mr Friabin at St Edith's Settlement…"

"I know him. I'll tell him."

By 9:30 am a flustered Toby was at the station. He was let in to the cell. "Five minutes," the guard constable said.

"Toby, what's this …?" Jimmy began plaintively.

"Now, my son, be calm and be quiet." Toby pointed at the ceiling and the walls. "All will be well. I swear it upon my life."

"But what's going on…?"

"The first opportunity we get to talk, my friend, will be at the remand prison, Brixton. I will be there. All will be told."

The rest of the day Jimmy was treated like a package; searched, stowed in a van to transport him to the court, dragged out, held in the cells until his case was called, prodded up the stairs to the dock. He confirmed his name to the magistrate, barely understanding that he was to be remanded in custody while the police pursued their enquiries. He was pushed downstairs, held in a cell, stowed in a van, transported to Brixton Prison and by 3pm, locked in a cell. He was dazed by the unexpectedness and the rapidity of events. He sat on the bed, his mind blank. He was not only incoherent; he didn't know what to say or to whom.

The following day, Jimmy was marched to a meeting room where lawyers see their remand clients. Toby was there, forcing a smile. They were under surveillance from outside but were able to talk confidentially, at least that was the belief.

"You said that about insurance, Toby…" Jimmy's first words were dry throated, thin and trembling.

"Indeed, and you will be pleased to know we are in good order in that direction, my son. I am sorry you have to be put through this." Toby moved his head close to Jimmy's and spoke in a very low voice. "But there has been a problem, as there often is where great men are concerned."

"Yeah," Jimmy replied depressively, his natural cynicism asserting itself. "In one word, Catesby."

"A temporary problem. News hounds are sniffing. Suffering extreme anxiety, the said Catesby has called upon his own insurers." Toby raised his arms and dropped them, signing that this was foreseeable.

"Who would they be?" Jimmy spat.

"The great and the good all over the land. I thought you knew that."

"Don't mess with me, Toby."

"Competing claims must be worked out, my lad."

"So whaddya mean?"

"The great Arnold Catesby cannot be charged, must not be charged. Another face must fit." Toby looked around at the rest of the empty room – only the eyes of the guard behind the glass. "Or shall we say, 'be fitted'," he added.

"Yeah, mine."

"No. Not you."

"But I've already been arrested on suspicion!"

"Hush, my friend. That's all it is, suss. The men in blue want to talk to you and no doubt intimidate you. Be ready for afternoon teas with Sneed, Turk and Hamish. Stick to your story. You won't be charged. In the meantime–"

"I'm gone!"

"Unruly horses have kicked over the traces. They will be reined in."

"So, who's goin' down for this?"

"A person yet to be chosen."

"By whom?"

"By our redoubtable guardians of the blue lamp."

"But it *is* fuckin Catesby! You know it, you seen it!"

"My warm friend, you must not have this rather literal regard for selected facts. Turn your mind to the more significant aspects of the case of poor Magdalena. Catesby is without question an intelligent, accomplished and distinguished man with much to bestow upon our nation. A truly worthwhile man. What a waste if he was sacrificed for a Polish whore, or an English whore if it comes to that. Unthinkable."

"Cut out the shit, Toby. Somebody else will be…"

"Selected. I judge the case cannot remain unsolved because it might just cause a festering unease among our trusty journos. Sooner or later, the information that there was a party at the Dog might ooze out. Nosey journos might look at the case if nobody is convicted. This must be avoided. A quick trial. Sentence. And finish.

Eternal silence."

"And it won't be me?"

"Trust me, Jim-boy, it won't be you."

As Jimmy watched Toby's large bulk from the rear, waddling toward the door, he had a feeling of loneliness and desolation.

Jimmy passed the monotonous routine on remand for two days, lying on his bunk listening to the voices, mumbling, raving; eating tasteless food sodden in fat, exercising half-heartedly in the yard. One inmate asked him what he was 'in for' and when he said 'murder', the man's eyes dilated with what looked like respect. Jimmy thought that there was no point in saying, 'I'm innocent'.

He was removed to the Jarndyce Street station twice, interviewed by Hamish and Sneed and shouted at by Turk, but he maintained his story. There was no other story.

Hamish only asked him whether he touched the body. Turk asserted that he did and that they had DNA evidence to prove it. Jimmy's thinking process and his usual line of back-chat failed him. All he could say was, 'That couldn't be true'. He said it over and over again as he watched Turk's temper rise. After four days he was taken to court and heard the police ask for an extension of time to complete their investigation. He was taken back to Brixton Prison and another round of questioning began. He repeated himself over and over and over again against the rising frustration of Turk and Sneed. Hamish had remained calm and somewhat distant.

He had been in custody for six days when a warder came to his cell door and said, "Visitor for you, Morton."

He led Jimmy to an interview room. There sitting demurely on a chair, ankles crossed was Josie. She shone like an exotic butterfly in the sombre room. The reversion to Martine Cleland was just about complete. Her pimples were gone. Her cheeks were smooth. Her hair remained short but was starting to wave, cultured waves of dark brown.

"Jimmy, dear." She stood up and came to him, touched his cheek with her lips. "I had to see you. This is terrible."

"Like I told you, Josie, I *saw* Eva's body on the night she was murdered, but that's all I know!" he blurted out, without invitation, what had now become a litany.

She fixed his eyes with a long, steady, shrewd glance. The whites of her grey eyes were clear. "You don't tell lies,

I know," she said, at last. "But what's going to happen?"

"I'm out of here soon, I hope."

"How can that be, Jimmy?"

"Don't ask me. I don't understand anyfink. I'm just a… nothin'."

"Arnold says the dicks have the evidence. He knows them."

"Christ, Josie, Catesby *did* it. I've seen the film. He's a crazy pervert. You know that already from what he tried on you."

"What do you mean you've seen the film?"

"The party was filmed by one of the girls."

She frowned, wide-eyed. "To sell?"

"Yeah, and Catesby bought it for a swag to save his scraggy neck."

"Surely the film doesn't show…"

"It shows Catesby coming out of a room with his trousers off and the girl zonked out on a couch behind him."

"*The girl* – Eva, you mean?"

"Yeah, Eva. With her dress up to her waist. I know what she was wearing that night."

"Are you sure? I mean…"

"Whaddya want, a full frontal?"

Martine sat still and silent, glassy-eyed.

"What about you? What are you doin' with Catesby?" Jimmy asked contemptuously.

Josie took no notice of his tone. "I've made a deal with him. Got a lawyer and that. It's a very big deal. He's sort of weakened. The Cleland Estate is going to get a fair price for the land.

"Weakened? I should think so, with murder on his mind. What about the shelter?"

"They'll be putting a dozer through it any time soon, clearing all the crap away."

"Crap. That's it then?"

"That's it. Oh, Jimmy… is there anything I can get you? I am going to get you one thing, a lawyer, so you can talk it over."

It was tempting, but he wanted to rely on Toby. If he got a lawyer he'd have to tell him everything and maybe that would cross up what Toby was doing. He shrugged and got up off the edge of the chair on which he had been sitting. Josie signaled the warder and kissed his cheek.

"I'll be in touch," she said, as the door clunked open. She strolled through it like a model on a catwalk, trailing her perfume and disappeared. He followed the warder to the remand cell. The cell door shut, a solid metallic impact. He placed his hand on the wall to steady himself, rigid with fear.

22

Hamish had a call from Turk. "We need to have a case-conference on Morton, Dan," Turk said in his loud, commanding voice.

"What's gone wrong?" Hamish said.

"Nothing, Dan, nothing, but we need to talk." Turk changed to a smoother gear.

That meant that something had gone wrong. "OK, I'll be in your patch around four. I'll come in."

Later in the day, Hamish went into the Jarndyce Street station and squeezed into Turk's office. Sneed was already there, crumpled in the corner with his eyes swiveling round like laser beams. Turk radiated a false bonhomie.

"We've been reviewing the Morton file, Dan, and we think maybe the evidence will be a bit light to get a conviction," Turk said.

"Sure, but we knew that when we decided to arrest him on suss," Hamish said. "He's involved. Mrs Thrussell says he handled the body. We can probably get forensic evidence to support that. If the evidence spills over into what happened at the party, he was admittedly in on the clean-up. He has some important questions to answer."

Hamish appreciated that the evidence to support a murder charge would have been weak, but at least a *prima facie* case for the jury. The Yard would have been pleased. He wouldn't be on active service when the case came to trial. He would of course be a witness, but if the prosecution failed, the failure would be academic as far as he was concerned. It couldn't hurt him. This was why he had recommended that Morton be arrested on suspicion, while the case was assembled to go forward to the Crown Prosecution Service. It was a matter of clearing the in-tray. Now, for no reason that he knew, Turk and presumably Sneed who moved in tandem, had changed their minds.

Turk seemed to be puzzled by Hamish's casual approach to the evidence but not displeased because it opened the way to consider other options. "Yes," he said, "but we haven't been able to screw anything in the way of an admission out of Morton. He's rock solid on his story. Ma Thrussell will say *he* placed the body, which she says was never in her place, by Johan's door. She's shaky. She mightn't live up to this in the witness box. And there is evidence by Emmett, the manager of the Shelter, that Morton was called out by Thrussell herself."

"Yeah," Hamish said. "We knew all that too, so why the change of mind?"

Hamish was conscious that he was giving Turk and Sneed the needle. They looked at each other, groped around, slack mouthed, for a moment. Hamish thought the sudden u-turn on Morton's guilt meant that Morton had a protector, somebody who had leaned on Turk and Sneed. Hamish could taste dirt, but he decided he wasn't going to resist Turk's argument.

Turk recovered himself quickly. He didn't want an issue with Hamish who was heading the investigation and entitled to call the shots. "We always review our cases, Dan. Bill will tell you we're very thorough. We've thought this through."

"It's taken a long time and with the kid in Brixton…"

"Better to be sure," Sneed said, "and a spell inside will

have done that little slimeball good. We were justified in holding him."

"So, who's the lucky contender for the chop? Catesby?" Hamish asked, wryly.

If he had been asked to give his candid assessment of guilt to anybody, he would have said Catesby, but candour was not a common coin in the force. He got from Rita Durbin a scent of the sex-with-violence which obsessed the man. Easy to go too far if you were that kind of man, especially with the added impetus of drugs. Eva had been very roughly handled. He guessed, and it could only be a guess, that Morton was a child sexually, compared to Catesby.

Turk seemed to relax when Hamish indicated he was prepared to look at another target. He beamed unconvincingly. "No chance with Catesby, Dan, whatever we might surmise. I take it you're joking."

"Sure," Hamish said readily. The folds of his face as smooth as if he was choosing a sandwich rather than a defendant on a charge of murder.

Proving a case against a suspected murderer categorically, the way that the star cop usually did in a whodunit, didn't come into Hamish's calculations. It was, according to him, facile to think that detectives proved cases in real life. Sometimes they got a genuine confession, or glaringly obvious evidence, but more often they went along with a stream of events. They scraped together circumstantial material which, on the face of it, appeared to suggest guilt. If they were lucky and the accused was unlucky, they had a win.

Although his own record of convictions in the cases that he had managed was not the best, it was well clear of any suggestion that he was asleep on the job. But if pressed on how many of his wins resulted in the conviction of the *truly* guilty person, he would have to concede that he couldn't be sure. The number of cases that came back to the courts years after the conviction and imprisonment of the supposed offender didn't surprise him at all. The criminal justice system was imperfect because human beings were imperfect. It would always be so, he thought.

"OK, agreed then," Turk said, in a deep voice, rubbing his big brown hands. "We'll all work on finding another contender."

23

Jimmy Morton was released from Brixton prison without ceremony after seven days of imprisonment. A warder came to his cell at 9am and said, "Right, Morton. You're outta here. Get your gear."

"Where'm I goin'?"

The warder hesitated and looked at him seriously, his face still. "Nowhere, I'd say."

Jimmy walked with the warder along the corridors toward the reception unit. "Get your other stuff over there." The warder pointed to a storage room. "Got the ticket?"

He was stood aside at the duty sergeant's desk while a call came through from Scotland Yard. The sergeant handed him the receiver. It was Hamish. "You're out, son. The charge has been withdrawn." Jimmy hung on to the receiver, speechless. "Are you there, Mr Morton? I want to inform you officially…"

"What charge?" Jimmy asked, finding his voice, dry and breaking.

Hamish chuckled softly. "Sorry, son. I should have said that the warrant has been withdrawn – " Jimmy handed the receiver back to the duty sergeant without replying.

Thirty minutes of slow formalities and slow inner gates later, Jimmy stepped into the sunlight outside the prison walls, his few clothes in a plastic bag. At the kerb was a late model black Mercedes saloon, very shiny, with the familiar figure of Toby Friabin lolling against it.

"Welcome back to paradise, my young friend." Toby opened the passenger door.

"Hiya, Toby," Jimmy said, very quietly, slinging his plastic bag on to the seat.

"It was bad in there, son?"

"The bed and food were OK. But it was a long time. And it was scary."

"Why scary? You'll have to excuse my ignorance but I've never experienced the delights of one of Her Majesty's prisons."

"Scary because *you don't know whether you'll get out,* Toby."

"My assurances, dear boy – "

"Fuck your assurances. A week is a long time!"

"I quite understand how you feel, lad." Toby conned the quiet car through the traffic with polished ease. "You just have to understand that there are a lot of cross-currents in the sea. I've kept my part of our bargain. Hamish rang me yesterday and told me he was withdrawing the warrant and arranging with the prison for your release."

"You persuaded Turk and Sneed?"

"Persuasion isn't the right word, Jimmy. Rather I'd say I asked for our contractual rights. We've looked after those two, and they have to look after us."

"Have to?"

"It's a solemn and binding contract. They break it at their peril."

"What peril?" Jimmy spat out the words.

"Loss of a nice little earner, disgrace from taking bribes, loss of job, loss of pension rights, prison. In that order."

"What about you? You'd be dragged in and others."

"You'd be surprised how well we cover our tracks in the jungle insurance business. And of course we think of the eventuality that a claim for cover isn't met, and what we might have to do."

"Who's 'we'?"

"Friends, Jimmy. I'll tell you more about it later."

"At least I'm out. Maybe they'll re-arrest me."

"No fear of that. Events have been moving while you've been away. You ought to come down to Pew Street and see."

"It's where I live, remember?"

"Not any more, son."

Jimmy stopped at Harry's Café and had bacon and eggs with Toby. Toby said, "I want to talk to you about your future, my friend, but not here. We'll meet at my penthouse tomorrow at ten. Have you got a pillow for your fair head tonight?"

"It's that bad, is it? Sure, I can sort something," Jimmy said, groping with the idea of coping with his future. "I didn't know that plans were so far advanced."

"Never mind plans. Action!"

He walked to Pew Street after the meal. All along the street, edging the footpath, sheets of board eight feet high had been erected. The boarding was painted a lavender colour. He passed a notice on the wall, a fancy sign with a silhouette of a castle with a coat of arms above it and the words 'Thirsten Group Developments'. The frontage of the building at Number 10 was still intact. He went inside. The lobby had been stripped of the receptionist's desk and was empty. He climbed the stairs. The shredded carpet runner had been removed; and the frames of Victorian etchings that had always been impossible to appreciate in the poor light.

The door to Kate's office was open. He could see her bending over a pile of files in cardboard envelopes. She heard him and looked up.

"Jimmy, you're back. Come in, come in!"

"Hi, Kate. Catesby on the move, is he?"

"Yes, I'll tell you about it but what about *you*? You've had an awful time."

"Yeah. Pretty lousy."

"Toby seemed to know what was happening. He's been keeping us in the picture. He said you'd be out soon. In fact, he said it at the last board meeting. I was surprised that the rest of the board, well the Ravens, took it so unenthusiastically, as though you were already guilty of something."

Jimmy gave a harsh, short laugh. He guessed Kate knew nothing of events around the murder. She might have known of the party at the Dog & Duck, but not the sinister implications. She certainly wouldn't know about Garnet's nest egg. She probably didn't know how he was involved and he said, "Betty Thrussell over at the Row called me over to shift Eva's body. I didn't touch it but that's how I got into this."

"Paul told me that. It was wicked of them to arrest you."

"Toby tells me the world is a wicked place." Jimmy had his amused old man look.

"There's something in that," Kate said ruefully. "A solicitor came here the other day, saying he had been instructed to act for you. He left this note." She handed him a slip of paper.

Jimmy took the paper. It was a solicitor's card, with 'Please call me' pencilled on it.

"He musta heard I was getting out."

He was suddenly conscious of the beat of heavy machinery and the clank of steel treads. He stood up and went to the window. It was much the same view as he had shared from his bedroom on the floor above, looking out toward Butchers' Row across the wasteland. In days the site had been transformed; it had been scraped clean. Demolition appeared to have started on the row of one block of tenements, the one where he used to live at the Thrussells'. The lavender boarding now enclosed what seemed a huge open space. Within that space, bulldozers and trucks were working with irascible energy.

"Jeez, Kate. I kinda knew this was coming up, but not like yesterday. What happened to the punters?"

"The homeless will always be around somewhere, but when something like this happens, they disappear like mice. They'll find their way to another shelter eventually. They won't be having a protest march in Pew Street."

"It looks as though those machines will soon be at the back door."

"They'll be knocking this place down soon. I'm afraid your room's been cleared, Jimmy, along with the rest of the rooms, except Paul's. He'll be here a day or two. I've had all your things packed and brought in here." She pointed to a box in the corner.

He thought that maybe they didn't expect him to come back, regardless of Toby's reassurances. It gave him a cold feeling in the pit of his stomach. "I ain't got much stuff. Guess I can find somewhere over at what's left of the Row. What about you, Kate? Where you gonna work?"

"I'm redundant. I've been paid off. Along with the rest of the staff. I have some money for you, too. Do you want me to go through it with you now?" She held out an envelope.

"Nah," he said, stuffing the envelope into the back pocket of his jeans. "That's St Edith's then?"

"Well, in a technical sense it will still exist. There's a pile of money from the buy-out here and the sale of the other building. The board will have to decide what to do. It's trust money. It'll have to go into something similar."

"Couldn't stop Catesby, huh?"

"I'm being paid enough not to even try."

"Josie, the woman I told you about, she coulda stopped him but she done a deal."

"Money, Jimmy, money."

Jimmy looked at her and then out of the window. "Gotcha."

24

Hamish was with Ed Turk, whose face shone like brass, and Bill Sneed in his soiled shirt, in Turk's office, while they summed up the possibility of a charge against Kevin Thrussell. The heater produced thick, hot, gaseous air.

The previous day, Hamish had questioned Thrussell. He had him brought to the Yard. Thrussell cowered, sweated and attempted bravado. He was ill at ease on the hard chair in a pale room, faced by Hamish's watchful but unthreatening scrutiny.

Hamish didn't feel sorry for Thrussell or pity him; he was a thug serving an apprenticeship as a career criminal. He knew he was looking at Thrussell from a distance and that wasn't quite fair but it was inevitable. He saw an uneducated and not very bright kid fighting to live, but fighting the wrong battles with the wrong people and yet stupid enough to believe he was absolutely right. Turk and Sneed had briefed him on the Butcher Boys, a violent and, in criminal terms, relatively successful gang of drug dealers and burglars, always fighting and sometimes dying, in internecine turf battles with other gangs.

Turk was at his most eloquent. "Thrussell's been digging a grave for himself with the Butcher Boys. In meddling with Eva's body he's jumped into that hole; and if he's tried for Eva's murder, he'll probably fill in the dirt over his head!"

"He won't look good at trial *if* he goes into the witness box," Hamish conceded. For the prosecutor and perhaps the judge it would be like bear baiting. "And there's some evidence of his actual guilt: a few hairs and threads from his clothing on the body," Hamish added with a tinge of scorn.

"Undeniable that he had handled the body," Sneed said.

"Thrussell's a satisfactory target. We'll get the little bastard," Turk said. "The evidence that he carried the body alive or dead across the road isn't helpful. The old guy who has given it is a demented alchoholic."

"No," Hamish said. "The reason that evidence is no good is because it opens up the possibility of a murder at the Dog & Duck with Thrussell merely the mortuary attendant."

Turk looked searchingly at Hamish, apparently irritated at this insight. "Sure," he said, reluctantly.

Hamish smiled slightly. "It would therefore point the finger at Catesby & Co. if it was used."

"We'll bin it then," Turk said. "Morton says the body was in Ma Thrussell's place. And we have a charge against the son whose traces are on the tart's clothing."

"Yes," Hamish said, "and the surmise story the prosecutor would have to put across is that the girl appears to have been picked up on Saturday night by Thrussell, *probably in the building* where she lived, taken to the Thrussell flat, assaulted and murdered and the body later moved presumably by him to the doorstep of the Tomachek flat.

"There's a few holes in it but not bad," Sneed said.

"A few holes?" Hamish said, "If it was a boat it would sink like a stone. Morton insists that Thrussell is innocent and that the killer is Catesby."

"What does that asswipe know?" Turk asserted.

Hamish persisted. "It doesn't matter if Morton is right or wrong, call him as a witness and he will say there was a sex party, including Eva, at the pub and the court will be want to know in detail what happened there."

"We'll trash Morton too and rely on the circumstantial," Turk said. "Simple and unanswerable."

Hamish reluctantly completed his file on the case in agreement with Turk and Sneed recommending the prosecution of Kevin Thrussell. "Yes," he said, "but a lot depends on how Thrussell plays it. You say the Butcher Boys are doing well. That means a smart mouthpiece for Thrussell. He'll hear the story and persuade Thrussell to admit he was paid to move the body from the Dog & Duck. Things will get very sticky then and names will be named."

"Nobody is going to believe the St Edith's board members are themselves involved," Turk said scornfully.

"No," Hamish grinned. "There'll just be a slight smell."

Hamish had more than a sense of the powers that were manipulating this case. Beneath the sleuthing there was another level of activity to which an honest detective like himself wasn't a party: the lies and deceit as worried or interested parties maneuvered to protect themselves and blame somebody else. This was a drama which took place in the shadows. Hamish could sense it and occasionally glimpse it, but he had learned to reflect and observe from afar and not intervene.

He could identify the manipulators: Catesby and his fellow board members who were at the party, Friabin, Turk and Sneed. Perhaps Durbin was paying a licence fee too that gave her leverage. She wouldn't want her business to be in the spotlight and Tomachek, equally. Each of these people certainly had something to hide, but Hamish knew that he would never know precisely what. It was obvious that Catesby and his friends would do everything to keep their whoring out of the newspapers, but even if the party was revealed, it would be well fenced with excuses that while the girls may not have been virtuous, the men were. The posh boys would live it down.

What Hamish *was* clear about was that all players were jostling to protect themselves and that the pressures they were putting upon each other were probably corrupt and illegal. Money would have been changing hands, but that would only be part of it. There would be threats, perhaps threats of violence, but more likely threats to reveal a past crime or some alternative evidence about Eva's murder.

"We can't fine tune the case. We'll just have to start it moving and see how it goes," Hamish said to Turk, who unctuously agreed, as he left the station.

25

Jimmy climbed the stairs of Number 10 to the third floor after leaving Kate. The door of Paul Emmett's room was open. Paul was seated at his desk surrounded by books and papers, his head in his hands. Two partly packed suitcases were open in the middle of the bare floor. Jimmy knocked. Paul's crew-cut head jerked up.

"Oh, you're back," he said. "I was beginning to worry that Friabin's sorcery wouldn't work."

"Yeah. Me too. A shit experience."

"Don't tell me. But you were in luxury. On remand."

He remembered that Paul was speaking from experience. "I ain't complainin' about the grub. It's the uncertainty. I didn't know anythin'." Jimmy's usually pasty face had a greenish tinge and he found it hard to smile. His infectious high spirits were low. Standing on the threshold of the room facing Paul, he looked malnourished, hollowed out by poverty and bad luck.

"Sit down on that chair. There's nowhere else. Your room's been emptied. They thought you weren't coming back."

"I guess a lot of people thought that. Well, I am bloody well back!" He sat on the creaking chair.

"That's the stuff. You're in the clear now?"

"Toby says. I'll get a bed over at the Row temporary and think about what I'm goin' to do."

"I've been thinking too, Jimmy. Look, I'm getting out

of Southwark. I might go somewhere up north, maybe Newcastle…" Paul was looking at the wall.

"What'll you do? I hear it ain't easy."

"I have contacts in the Church. They'll treat me as a wounded war veteran. They'll find me a place to live and a job."

"Doing what?"

"Maybe like I've been doing here or adult teaching – I can't work with kids." He swung around to face Jimmy. There was tension and anxiety in his voice. "Why don't you come with me? We can get a place together. I'll get you a job. Something better than the grubby way you live now…"

Jimmy intervened firmly but not coldly. "I like it, Paul. I been happy. OK, it's over, but I just wanted to say that."

Paul's eyes looked blind, black and white beads. "*Happy*. All right. Don't you feel demeaned when you beg?"

Jimmy's eyes gleamed. "No way. I'm touchin' people's hearts as well as their pockets. They get a hit! I'm jiggin' a little muscle that they don't use much." He laughed for the first time.

"St Bernard's is a fraud."

"You told me everything is a fraud. And I believed you. So what does it matter?"

Paul bent his head condescendingly like a wise and liberal academic. "But you have to *do* something, Jimmy. You show very good capabilities. If we're together we can develop those. I want to do it. I can get you ready for exams that will qualify you…" He spoke with sincerity.

Jimmy understood that Paul had dreams for him, yes, real dreams, wanted to make him into something, Jimmy wasn't sure what. He understood that the product of Paul's dreams would be beneficial to him, highly beneficial, but he said, "It'll take a long time. I ain't *that* good."

"You're underestimating yourself. And what's a bit of time? It'll be worth it."

"It's a very big offer, Paul, and I want to think about it…" Jimmy was grateful, but wary of being controlled or getting into intimacies which were so demanding that he couldn't decently refuse proposals. He wasn't thinking about sex. That had been dealt with conclusively. He was thinking about the direction of his life from here on.

"We've been good friends working here together, haven't we? You'll be your own man," Paul said, appearing to intuit what Jimmy was thinking.

Jimmy was sceptical. Paul was dominating – not that he tried to dominate; it was the natural result of a powerful mind. He was a hard man to refuse. It would be difficult to admit that to Paul. Instead, he said, "Sure. That's not it. Only I got my own ideas what I wanta do." He didn't know if he could explain.

Paul gave him a slightly surprised look. "OK. What?"

"Probably go to Australia for a few months. Look around. Come back and emigrate." It came out easily, simply.

Paul sat up stiffly. "What are you looking for?"

"Wife, family, job where I'm boss." Again, Jimmy was formulating thoughts he'd had for a long time but never clearly expressed.

"You can get those anywhere," Paul said, scornfully. "You don't have to go to Kangaroo-Land to get them."

"Maybe. I just have an idea I'd like to have those things where the sunshine is."

"It's an illusion, Jimmy. *Sunshine*? Sunshine is in the head and the heart, not in the sky."

"My head tells me it's in the Australian sky. My heart

says that's the brand I want," Jimmy grinned, determined not to be serious, fearing that if he was, he would be drawn into Paul's spell.

"You're kidding yourself. Don't you get it? Each of us is alone and responsible for ourselves, because nobody else is. You can't know anybody else, not one single human being, not your wife, not your children and there's nothing out there. Nothing."

Jimmy felt like joking 'You mean Australia isn't there?' but Paul's grey skin and sightless eyes unnerved him. He said, "I'll buy all that, but it doesn't mean you can't have fun."

"There isn't any fun, Jimmy. There's only darkness and the canker of your own corruption and broken dreams."

"Maybe darkness for you, but fun for me. You did a bad thing, Paul, and it burns you. I don't know why it burns you if there's nothin' out there. If it's all nothin', nothin' matters. Why bother to remember it? Why bother to suffer?"

Paul tried to pull his mouth into a semblance of cordiality, his stiff lips withdrawing to reveal his teeth. "You're a more convincing nihilist than I am!"

"A what?" Jimmy asked lightly.

"Jimmy, come with me. I need you," Paul said in a low voice, his head sagged down.

"I better go now, Paul, I gotta organise my dosser." He crossed the floor, again feeling like a priest himself. He put his hand on Paul's shoulder. He saw the tears Paul was trying to hide. "I'll let you know tomorrow morning."

26

Jimmy collected his books and clothes from Kate's office. They weren't bulky but he had to carry them the long way, along Pew Street to Butchers' Row, instead of cutting across the wasteland which now had closed gates.

The publican at the Dog & Duck, where he had occasionally pulled pints in the past, was pleased to have him on the night staff. Jimmy was good with the customers. He let Jimmy have a staff bedroom. The room looked out on the wheelie bins and Jimmy thought he could smell them. He dumped his belongings on the bed and went to the bar. He ordered a pork pie and salad and washed it down with a beer. He had to fend off a few of the regulars who were curious about his reappearance. "Cops made a fuckin' mistake, din't they?" he repeated, always in his buoyant manner.

When he went back to his room, he washed up in the staff bathroom and went to bed. He thought about Paul's offer to live with him. Paul was right. Paul could teach him a lot. And he liked Paul. But going to Newcastle? Jimmy had never been there. He had heard it rained a lot and things were tough. It seemed like going to a monastery. It wouldn't be much fun; it would be serious. Sure, Paul wouldn't consciously exercise any constraint on him, but Paul's presence and advice would be an implicit constraint. It seemed an unattractive move, advantageous as it could be – he could probably get a qualification and a good job.

He slept fitfully and tossed these thoughts around. In the morning, as he ate bacon and eggs in the bar, his mind was more on how to explain himself to Paul. The relationship between them was sensitive and he couldn't just refuse Paul and say that was that. He wanted to say 'no' in a decent way, a way that wouldn't offend Paul.

It was after 8am when he started to walk to Number 10 Pew St. As he went by the fence he could hear the coughing and growling of the trucks and dozers behind. Coming upon the entrance to the building suddenly, where the lavender fence was parted by the façade of St Edith's, made it seem like the entrance to a mysterious garden. When he went inside it was a dusty and deserted cave. Before the earthworks had started, the old pile had a smudged identity. He could feel St Edith's had a small, almost embarrassed purpose, embarrassed because it was failing. Not now. It *had* failed. It was a ruin. Upstairs, he passed Kate's office and he was surprised to see her there again, her hair falling down to shroud her, as she bent her shoulders over the desk in her grey, tent-like dress.

"Just goin' up to see Paul," he said, and she looked up and beckoned him inside.

"I've got your paperwork here, Jimmy," she said. "The severance pay has gone into your bank account. And I gave you the back pay in cash, yesterday. Have you made any plans for the future?"

Jimmy pushed the papers in his pocket without looking at them. "I'll still be workin' on St Bernard's. Toby's fixed up an office at his yard. And stayin' over at the Dog."

"Yes, Toby told me about St Bernard's." She had a strained smile. "Good luck with it, and… try to get something else. You can, you know. You don't want me to go through the pay figures with you?"

"Nah, Kate, thanks. You'll make it right." He went on up the stairs.

He couldn't understand how, in a week, the third floor could have aged half a century. His own room seemed impossibly small, with the bed and chair and his box of belongings removed. The damp stains and peeling wallpaper which he'd hardly noticed before, were obtrusive. The bare, board floors in the passage were dirty, uneven and rotting in places. The ceilings sagged.

The door of Paul's room was open. He went in. The half-packed suitcases were still open on the floor. Paul wasn't there. He saw that the desk was littered with papers Paul had been sorting. He noticed the bed was neatly made; Paul was always up early. He tried to connect last night with this morning. Nothing seemed to have changed, except that the night had gone and the day had come. He had a flicker of anxiety. He walked to the door. He listened. He could hear the bulldozers. He looked down the passage. He couldn't hear any noises from the bathroom. Paul might have left the building, but he wouldn't have left the door open and his papers scattered around; he was too orderly in his habits for that. Jimmy decided he must be in the bathroom. He stepped along the hall.

"You in there, mate?" he said, as he stuck his head in the opening of the door which had no workable lock.

The room was brightly lit by the low sun piercing the cracked frosted glass of a small window. To one side, a chair lay on its back on the tiles. A long, dark column was scribed from the ceiling, almost to the floor, against the glaring background. It was a moment before his sight adjusted. A body was hanging by a cord knotted to a pipe in the ceiling.

He crossed the threshold and went closer. In death and

suspended, Paul looked like one of those agonised, reedy figures he had seen on Roman Catholic icons.

When Kate reported the death to the duty officer at the Jarndyce Street station, Ed Turk came on the line. She said, "I think it's suicide. We haven't touched the body."

"You and Morton stay put until we get there," he said.

During the time that it took the police to arrive, Kate, red-eyed, went on with her packing. Jimmy watched from the window as the dozers and trucks fed on the corpse of St Edith's bonfire space like hungry ants. He weighed how much his rebuff of Paul had led to this. Paul had the insight to see that Jimmy had already decided to refuse to go with him to Newcastle. Jimmy hadn't intended to be that obvious. In truth, he hadn't made up his mind precisely. He hadn't intended to brush Paul off this morning. He had rehearsed a dozen phrases which he intended to use. They could have remained friends and seen each other occasionally. And he hadn't realised how important he was to Paul; that was a jolt alongside the sickening shock of death. To think that his decision to push on alone could precipitate the death of a friend was crushing; it made him question his own understanding of Paul.

"Do you know why Paul did this, Jimmy?" Kate asked.

"I more or less told him last night I couldn't go to Newcastle with him."

"I know he was fond of you. Don't blame yourself. It was probably a number of things. Loss of his job. And he was a very depressed man."

A cruiser full of cops arrived after an hour, yielding Sneed, two forensic specialists and Hamish. After the bathroom and Paul's room had been examined and Kate questioned,

Hamish interviewed Jimmy standing up in the privacy of his old room.

"Bit cramped, isn't it? Bet you're glad to get out," Hamish said. "Can you tell me why Mr Emmett did this? I'm assuming it was suicide."

"He ran out of road."

"Sure. Why?"

"He didn't believe in anythin' so he didn't have anythin' to lose. He was a friend. We worked together. He talked to me."

Hamish thought about this. "You were probably the last person to see him alive last night, did you realise what he planned?"

"No. Not a clue. He planned to go to Newcastle and he asked me to think about joining him."

"This is a small community around Butchers' Row. Did he know Eva Walecka?"

"I dunno."

"Did he ever refer to her in a critical or offensive way. Was he angry with her?"

"If you're thinkin' he might have dunnit, you're on the wrong horse."

"Why? Some people have strong, sometimes uncontrollable feelings about prostitutes."

"He was here, in this building on the night and Eva was killed over at the Dog & Duck."

"How do you know where Eva was killed?"

"I worked it out. You must know more than I do, so you should have worked it out."

Hamish liked Morton's calm affability and directness. "Who killed her?"

"Catesby."

"Why choose him from the others?"

“He thinks women are bits of meat to be fucked and throttled.”

“How can you know that?”

“He tried it on with the girls here at St Edith’s.”

Hamish already knew about Catesby’s antics at St Edith’s from Kate Martin, but even with the Employment Tribunal cases and Martine Cleland’s lack of frankness there was nothing conclusive in any way.

“When’ll you arrest Catesby?” Jimmy asked

“There’s no evidence against Sir Arnold Catesby.”

Jimmy was feeling low and his usually equable temper was disturbed. “C’mon, if that was a party at the Dog with me an’ me mates, we’d be in the jug already!”

“I understand how you feel…”

“No, you don’t. Pushed around, pushed around like a bit of shit. Slammed into clink an’ I ain’t done nuthin!”

“What makes you so certain that it’s Catesby, Mr Morton? You haven’t told me anything that really connects him…”

Jimmy was alight, his chest and face burning. It was against all his rules to step into other people’s disputes, but he couldn’t stop himself. “I seen a film taken on the pub night!”

Hamish moved back. His face contracted into a network of lines. “I see… but is there anything but a raunchy party in the film?”

Jimmy was certain he was talking himself into strife, but there was still a hot part of him that wanted to go on. “Catesby with his prick out and Eva looking like dead on a couch behind him.”

“Where is the film, Mr Morton?”

“Catesby bought it.”

“Who sold it?”

"I dunno."

"Who took the film? One of the women?"

Jimmy paused. He couldn't say he didn't know. How could he know about the existence of the film? "Somebody maybe pissed off with being groped," he began uncertainly.

"Who told you about the film?"

"Pub talk around here."

"Where was the film shown?"

"In the bar of the pub." He'd given plenty away already and was beginning to feel the chill of having said too much.

"Who organised that?"

"I dunno. There was a crowd."

"Thanks for the help, Mr Morton. You should have told me before."

"I didden' know until the other day... You're the sleuth, not me. An' you were goin' to pin it on *me*."

27

Hamish wanted to think about Morton's revelation. Could he believe it? He strolled to Harry's Café, frequently mentioned by the witnesses he had interviewed. It was tiny, busy at the counter with sales of take-away pastries. He ordered a custard cake and a coffee which he could see in advance was going to be the boiled black water variety. Harry, a Vietnamese man, had no espresso machine.

He sat down at a cramped table by the window. Harry's helper, a small, frowning, brown-skinned woman swathed in what looked like a grubby patchwork quilt, was clearing tables. She fired the dirty plates and cutlery into a plastic bin, staccato gunshots which shattered Hamish's thoughts.

When they spoke earlier, Morton was mourning the death of his friend and he had just been released from Brixton which he understandably resented. He was sore and on edge. The silence, which was second nature to him, had slipped, if only for a few seconds, before reasserting itself in lies and evasions. But it had slipped. Yes, Hamish could believe there was a film. Morton was a fly character, but there was no point in him fabricating a story about the film to deflect suspicion from himself. Hamish had already put him in the clear.

And who took the film? Hamish thought he could work that out. His bet was Garnet Peabody. Rita Durbin was a woman plying her lucrative business. Gloria Thrussell was dumb and motiveless. Garnet Peabody was a sharp girl with a motive. Her complaints against Catesby, for which Kate Martin could get her no relief, reached back many months. Time to build up her anger and resentment.

If the Crown went to trial with a film as explicit as Morton said, a conviction against Catesby was virtually guaranteed. It would be desirable for the prosecution to show how the body travelled across the road, but even that became less important. The supposition would be that Catesby had ordered its disposal.

If it was true that Catesby bought the film, a large sum of money would have been paid. That could be traced by recourse to bank records. The problem of getting authority and the opportunity to delve into the bank records was a difficult, probably impossible, one. Catesby and his friends would deny any knowledge. Pressing them would be useless and even counter-productive; they would claim they were being victimised. And the transaction would have been effected through intermediaries by men who lived in a world of cash flows.

Garnet Peabody would obviously deny she knew anything about a film, but he might be able to budge her. Before talking to her he could order a search of her home, more a way of unsettling her than in the hope of finding a copy of the film or any tangible evidence about it. Hamish concluded that the possibility of finding a copy of the film was very remote indeed.

Hamish washed down the tasty and light pastry of his custard cake with the cooled thin coffee. He considered the furore his investigation of this lead would cause and the sheer complexity of it, balanced against the remote chance of success. He wiped his mouth with the paper napkin and rose from his chair, clear in his mind that he would take no immediate action to uncover the film. On his way out, he smiled stiffly at the waitress who was still recovering plates to crash. He wondered whether the din had influenced his difficult decision.

Hamish spent the rest of the day with the case file at his Scotland Yard office. One of the detective-sergeants on his team, in the course of enquiries in Butchers' Row, had ploughed up a useful, perhaps vital, piece of information. The routine question he asked regulars at the Dog & Duck, and some inhabitants of what was left of the accommodation in the street, was whether they had noticed anything unusual on the party night. The detective was equipped with photographs of all players – members of the board, Friabin, Kevin Thrussell, Tomachek, Jimmy Morton and the four women. He noted that all except the board members were known by sight to many of the locals. Friabin and Morton's late night visit to the Dog was confirmed by three people who had seen them. And one witness claimed that he had seen Kevin Thrussell helping a drunken girl across the road to Butchers' Row at a time which could be fixed as earlier than the visit to the Dog by Friabin and Morton. According to the locals, Butchers' Row was a lively social scene until well after midnight on Saturdays.

Hamish began to think how this linked up with another piece of information which hadn't seemed significant. Detective Sneed who was a bottom feeder, very much a party to community gossip, had told him that Rita Durbin and Kevin were an item. 'Funny thing going on there,' Sneed had said. 'Rita's soft on him. She isn't bad looking, but she's twice his age. She's got money, mind. Doesn't bother with grown men, except for business'. Hamish thought that perhaps the way to tackle the Thrussell sighting was through Rita Durbin. He asked her to call at the Jarndyce St station the following day.

Hamish and Sneed saw her in one of the bleak interview rooms. Her face wasn't made up; the skin was yellow and waxy. She had lost her eyebrows. Wrinkles showed around her pursed lips. Hamish started with her in his usual pleasant low key. "Rita, we have a reliable witness, who says he saw Kevin Thrussell, whom he knows by sight, helping a drunken girl cross the Row from the Dog before midnight on the Saturday. 'Helping' could be carrying. 'Drunk' could be dead."

"Why tell me?" Rita Durbin snapped.

"You know Thrussell. Did you see him on the premises at the Dog, or in the street, or elsewhere at about this time?"

"No. He wasn't around."

"You're sure?"

"He wasn't around when I left."

"And when you left, everything was OK at the Dog? No murder. Eva was there."

"I'm not sure. I wouldn't have known. I was in one room; the others were in other rooms."

"Did you speak to Thrussell that night either personally or communicate electronically?"

Rita Durbin raised her hoarse voice: "Kevin Thrussell's no killer. He may be a bit wild, but he's a kid. From what I hear, Eva was killed by a pervert!"

"Answer my question."

She hesitated, her eyes darting erratically as though the answer could be found in the tight little room. "I invited him on my mobile and he stayed at my place."

"You're soft on Kevin, aren't you?"

"Kevin Thrussell didn't do this."

"Who did, Rita?"

Rita Durbin smoothed her hand across her brow, her eyes on the carpet tiles. "I don't know. What about Johan

Tomachek? This was just what that scumbag could do."

"He wasn't here. He has an alibi."

"He *was* here. He may have got himself an alibi, but he was here. He would have been very rough with Eva if she was moonlighting, thinking he was away. I saw him in the street as I went home that night."

"We'll check on his story again."

Hamish could see a dark hole in Durbin's testimony about the state of affairs when she left the Dog. She was lying, he thought, to protect herself. Well, that was to be expected. She didn't want to talk, because if she did, she would be the star witness in a very sensational case and her name, her work and her picture would be all over the news media. But it left her lover, Kevin exposed. She couldn't go far enough to protect him without harming herself. And maybe she had something to fear from the murderer. Catesby, for example, wasn't within the usual definition of a crook, but he could reach out to her through his minions.

Hamish didn't mess with niceties about Kevin Thrussell. A member of his squad picked Thrussell up in the street an hour later and offered him the opportunity to visit the Yard in the cop car freely or be arrested on suspicion of murder. Thrussell went quietly.

"Your name keeps coming up in the Eva Walecka murder enquiry, Mr Thrussell," Hamish said as they settled in the interview room. "Tell me again what you know."

Thrussell couldn't hide the sweat on his face. "I had nuffin' to do with it. I already told you."

"A witness saw you in Butchers' Row on the Saturday night with a drunk or maybe a dead woman."

"Not me. I was in Brixton."

"Your DNA is on Eva's dress."

"Not mine. It's a stitch-up!" Thrussell shouted aggressively.

"It's a scientific fact. Did you speak with Rita Durbin that night?" Hamish went on calmly.

"Naah, why should I?"

"Where did you sleep that night?"

"Brixton. With mates."

"Rita Durbin says you slept at her apartment."

"She's lyin'."

Hamish took a long, expressionless look at Thrussell and moved his head in disbelief. "Think of what you're saying, Mr Thrussell. You're likely to be charged with murder. You can't get around the DNA evidence. Alibis and denials are not going to impress a jury. If you try to change your story at the last moment, it'll look bad. Better to tell the truth now."

"I already told you."

Hamish had the impression that Thrussell was gritting his teeth and saying what he had been told to say. In this, in his own paltry way, Thrussell was no different than Catesby and Co.

28

Jimmy visited Toby's penthouse as promised at 10am in the morning and was admitted through the steel door with warm greetings from Toby. In the kaleidoscopic colours of the lounge, he found Amethyst waiting with a cup of tea and a plate of cream cakes. They settled down on the couches around the low table, and with little other than the occasional quip, they emptied the plate. When they had finished, Toby leaned back, brushing the crumbs and flecks of cream around his lips away with the back of his hand.

"My boy, this is a propitious moment…"

"Toby, I didn't want to say anythin' that might have spoiled the cakes, but Paul has topped himself."

"My dearest," Toby said to Amethyst, "why don't you leave us while we deal with this unfortunate news."

Amethyst nodded dumbly, gathered the cups and plates and left the room.

"I found him hanging in the bathroom this morning."

"Do we know why? Surely his job as manager wasn't *that* vital?"

"I only know what I seen."

"Nice chap, our Paul. Never did understand him myself." Toby's face smoothed over and his eyes seemed to be looking inward.

Jimmy thought of the *nothing* which Paul had often talked about. He had left a space like a hole in the air in Jimmy's life. The two men sat with their own unexpressed thoughts, an impromptu moment of silence for Paul.

Toby coughed. "One more nasty thing, my boy, before we get to the good news. I was quietly making my way to Harry's Caf yesterday morning, passing a parked ultramarine Bentley, somewhat rare in the neighbourhood, when the driver accosts me. He hops out and swings open the passenger door. 'Why not join my guv'nor inside?' he says. And there, hidden by smoked glass and reclining on soft cushions with a face as stiff as a copper frying pan is the delightful Catesby.

"'To what, or to whom, do I owe the honour of this visit,' I say, getting in.

"'You owe it to your own lying self, Friabin,' Catesby says, closing the glass partition from his driver. 'I want a very private word with you because your future is in doubt.'

"'Delighted to oblige,' says I, 'because I thought my future was assured.' I felt a chill of panic, my lad, but tried to make light of it.

"'You can get the smirk off your face, Friabin,' he says in that silky voice. 'I had a visit from Hamish. He tells me that lout Thrussell is to be charged. And it's watertight. *He says.* He says the police will be prosecuting on the basis that the crime occurred in the tenement where Thrussell's mother lives. I want to be quite sure that everything you say and do will be consistent with that.'

"Feeling damp in my armpits, I say, 'Sir, I would not dream of revealing your innocent frolics at the Dog.'

"Catesby swings his head to look at this lowly creature. I face the pupils of his eyes, two mirrors in which I fancy I can see myself quivering.

"'You remember our previous conversation, Friabin?' he snarls.

"'Most certainly, sir, every word, every intonation, every nuance.'

"'If this matter surfaces, you clown, I shall press the button, your button, without further talk. Is that clear?'

"'As a well-polished showroom window, my lord,' I say. 'And may I congratulate you on your recent ennoblement.'

"'Get out, you jackass!' he shouts, and I tumble out of that aromatic hide interior on to our unlovely street."

"Hamish's got it all wrong, Toby, if that's the way he's going."

"I agree my dear boy, but who am I to contest the will of the mighty Catesby? And who knows which way Hamish will go when he goes?"

Jimmy realised Toby was under pressure and regretted what he had told Hamish about the film, because in a sense it betrayed Toby. He could see that if Hamish cared to investigate that avenue, Toby, never mind Catesby, might have a lot of questions to answer and even criminal charges. And Toby would have to face Catesby carrying out his threat.

Jimmy had spoken to Hamish in anger, a rage against the protective shield that Catesby had around himself and his friends. But the shield was there, it was a fact, just as his own insurance was a fact. His words had been blurted out; but he couldn't face revealing his betrayal to Toby.

"Jim-boy, let us get on to infinitely more pleasant things," Toby said, breaking into Jimmy's thoughts. "The purpose of our meeting, no less. I've been thinking of your future my son, and your undoubted skills. Do you know you are the best collector of the whole bunch?"

"No, but I done well for myself. I know that."

"James, I have two fine options for your future. One is St Bernard's. You come off the street and manage the whole shebang. About twenty collectors now and as many more as you want to recruit and train."

"That sounds easy, Toby," Jimmy said with a touch of

suspicion. "Recruit a team. Run them. Count the lolly. I can do that standing on one leg."

"Indeed, you can. It's why I want you. And there's more, of course. You would have to manage the fund, pay our insurance and collect other contributions from honest businessmen."

"I would be paying cops and councillors… and collecting protection money?"

"Dealing with worthies for, or from whom, a small donation was appropriate."

"But how would I fix the numbers?"

"You would work with a small management group, including my goodself. You would gain experience. You would eventually look Mr Turk in the eye and tell him what he's entitled to and what you want in return."

"Sounds… dangerous."

"Never. All risks covered."

"Why me, Toby?"

"Because you are a very able man and I need a partner. I'm not well, Jimmy. I need someone there who is capable and who I can trust."

Jimmy had never fancied himself as a Mr Big behind the scenes, never even thought of it. "I'll have to think about it Toby. Sounds very difficult."

"It is complex and shall we say delicate. I believe you can develop the qualities."

"The dosh?"

"As much as the director of a top City company. We are talking over a hundred thousand to start."

"Jeez! Includes drug business?"

"No. It's purely financial."

"Uh-huh," Jimmy said slowly "…that's good. What else were you going to say?"

"Tempting Jim-boy? The other thought I had was my used car business. You would be a partner and take a cut on every car. I grew up in the veg market, Jimmy. I know a salesman when I see one. You're a natural. You'd learn to do the auctions too. Plenty of mazuma there."

"Some of the cars have been boosted?"

"Not all of them. You'd be buying and selling often from and to the ordinary honest man in the street – that is assuming there are such people."

"All doctored?"

"The stall-boy polishes his fruit, Jimmy. Let's say our products are shined and adjusted to show their best qualities. You wouldn't be involved in any of this. Overnight, for a fee, your bent Porsche becomes a shiny low-mileage dream car."

Jimmy had no fear that Toby would use him to do things Toby wouldn't do himself. And he had no concern about the genuineness of the offers in monetary terms. But he didn't like either offer much. Handling bribes was fearsome. He could do ten or fifteen years in the cooler for that. He accepted what Toby said about risks being covered, but what that implied was, if anything went seriously wrong, the case would be big and bruising and he would be at ground zero. But flogging cars was at least tempting. It was tainted, sure but relatively small beer. Like the supermarket wine it was 'us against them'. Two or three years of that and he could quit with a packet and get out of town.

He decided to get some time by playing one offer off against the other. "I can't decide now, Toby. I'm kinda torn between. I'll get back to you. I never thought of myself as your partner…"

"You deserve it, son. Take all the time you need."

29

Jimmy visited Josie at her apartment, once or maybe twice a week, always at her insistence and by her calling him on his mobile. He never initiated the visits. She even returned to begging with him on rare occasions. She pretended it was a lark, but he wasn't fooled. She kept an outfit of old clothes to wear. She seemed desperate to win his favour, which surprised him. She began to buy him gifts of clothes, garments he'd never had before because he never had the need for them: soft moccasins, a cashmere sweater, designer jeans. When she presented him with a leather jacket, he said, "Hey, whaddya think I am, a goddam film star?" but couldn't help being pleased. It was a lovely jacket and he didn't hesitate to wear it.

"I've got money, Jimmy and I'm happy to share it with you. It gives me pleasure."

He waved a relaxed hand of acceptance. "And you got a brief on the job when I was jugged. Thanks for that. I never needed him, fortunately."

"I would have paid for your defence, gladly."

"If I'd been tried, I'd never have gotten away," he said reflectively. "However smart the brief."

"Why say that?" she frowned. "You told me you had nothing to do with it."

"Right on. Not a damn thing to do with it, but I would have been stitched up tight. Your man Mr Catesby likes a neat job."

"Now, Sir Arnold Catesby by the way. He couldn't do that, Jimmy."

"You think you know what wags the world, Josie. I'm tellin' you, he could and nearly did. Some other poor bugger will have to suffer."

"How did you get out?"

He drew a slow inward breath. "Mates…"

"You've got powerful friends, Jimmy."

"You wanta be careful of Catesby, Josie. He's a violent sex pervert. You know that. What you told me? How he lost it with you?"

She moved her shoulders uncertainly. "Maybe." Then she smiled, reached under a cushion on the couch, and produced a small, snub-nosed Colt revolver, pointing it at Jimmy. "I've got protection."

"Hey," he said, startled, "put that away." He was used to seeing firearms handed around but not by Josie.

After a long pause, she returned to a subject she had more than hinted at before. "Why don't you stay here, Jimmy. Live here, with me?"

Josie was still in the same apartment she had rented in Butchers' Row. She had had the interior painted in an off-white colour. It was comfortable and spacious but the Victorian skyline of the neighbourhood was crumbling and out-of-doors there was a foreboding of destruction and violent change.

"I know you've got the king-size bed," he laughed.

"I got it for you. Why do you think I'm still here?"

"I been wonderin'. You're a stylish doll now. You made your deal. You got the moolah. You could move uptown any time."

"I came here, I guess for protection, when I couldn't think straight. When I could think, I wanted to find out what Arnold was up to. Now I want to be here… so I can see you."

He could see it was difficult for her to say this. "OK. Look, I like you a lot, Josie. You're a friend and… it's great in bed."

"Is that all, Jimmy?" Her eyes were scarlet rimmed.

He hesitated. He didn't want to say, 'Yes, that is all.' But he knew he should. Instead, he tried to explain. "You belong in a different life from mine. You're Martine Cleland, a rich broad. You been everywhere an' seen everythin'. Doors open for you. How couldya settle down with a guy who runs a bicycle shop in Port Douglas?"

"I don't even know where Port Douglas is, but I could settle down with you Jimmy, I could, I could and I want to!" She flung herself at him, wrapped her arms around him so forcefully that he staggered backwards.

The embrace wasn't sexy or even affectionate; it was a cry for shelter. He grasped her shoulders and pushed her away. "Hell, be sensible, Josie. You'd get tired. You'd want the old life: cars, restaurants, cruises, resorts, after a while. An' you'd say to me, 'Why not, I have the money?' Like the leather jacket. An' what could I say? Nuthin'."

"What's wrong with cars and restaurants and resorts, Jimmy. Isn't that what you're working for?"

"Thing is, I want my own sort of life *made* by me. A life is like a house; it's gotta be constructed. Course you can buy one off the peg, swallow somebody else's plans. An' different people got different toolkits. I don't wanna be a poodle in anybody else's kennel." His metaphors and similes tripped over each other and faded away.

"Silly macho pride! I'll give the whole fucking estate away. I'll give it all to charity!"

"That's not the answer, Josie. I reckon you know it. Look

I'll tell you what we'll do. We'll send out for a Chinese, have a bloody great whisky each and make love."

Jimmy couldn't articulate his precise feelings for Josie. Not because he couldn't divine his own feelings, but because the whole truth was shocking, unmentionable. What he had told her was quite true as far as it went; their life experience was so vastly different that it would be hard to bridge. Josie could understand that. No, there was something else. Josie had plumbed heartless depths as an addict and a whore which he could never understand or accept. He found that aspect of Josie repellent; he who had lived so near the edge of those depths himself. There was a small door in his mind that was closed as far as Josie was concerned.

He had considered it a lot. It wasn't a matter of forgetting her rotten experience and concentrating on the pleasure, the personal advantage of being subbed by a rich bird and the future financial potential of their relationship. He didn't regard her as blameworthy. What had happened to her was almost an obvious train of events. But the end result was that she had a brown spot like an overripe peach. She couldn't start any warmly affectionate or romantic feelings in him. Paul would have said she had a touch of rot.

He applied for a passport and bought himself a return economy flight to Australia. He passed the days by working the St Bernard's tins. He'd let Toby know the answer about the job offers when he came back from Aussie. Toby didn't like this; he probably realised the answer was 'no' on both options, but his good spirits were undimmed. "Like a bride deserted at the altar, I will remain in hope," he said.

Jimmy kept an eye on the progress of the work around Number 10 Pew Street; it interested him. He didn't want it to disappear but he had to watch the inevitable. The St

Edith's building was now deserted and boarded up. He could actually view the area from the top floor of the Dog & Duck, the rooms where he believed Eva had been murdered. He climbed the stairs each morning before he went begging. From here he could look across Butchers' Row. The tenements where Ma Thrussell lived had already been demolished and he had a clear sight of the patch over the lavender fence. The bulldozers had finished clearing and were gouging out a vast pit for the bed of the new skyscraper. Tall cranes pecked like cruel birds as they hoisted steelwork for the foundations.

St Edith's looked forlorn at the edge of this clay desert with its iron insects, the red bricks blackened by time. He could get a clearer view of the whole structure now that it stood on its own, exposing the brickwork and plaster intricacies which adorned Victorian red brick architecture, the little turrets, the ledges and ornate chimneys and panels around the windows.

He tried to imagine St Edith's 150 years ago, standing proudly in a terraced row of smart town houses, not quite a church but almost. Paul had explained the history; so many hopes to spread the word of a good life had burned brightly, then flickered and died out.

One morning he saw that St Edith's had been dynamited; it was not flattened, but mortally wounded, crumbled to a pile littered with fragments of walls and broken chimneys. Bulldozers were beginning to scrape up the bricks in clouds of dust. Very soon, perhaps by dark, Number 10 would be a memory and a few more yards of lavender panel-board would replace the gap in the frontage.

30

Hamish had a low-key farewell party at Scotland Yard which was well attended. He was a popular man. Two chiefs at different stages in his career were there and made warm speeches. Words like 'capable', 'careful', 'sensitive', 'supportive', 'fair' and 'good humoured' were used to describe him. He received a gold-plated fountain pen inscribed with his initials and the dates of his service as a present. It was a nice thing to have; he thought wryly that in the age of the iPad and the smartphone it was a relic, like his career. Hamish gave a light-hearted reply and told a mildly funny, carefully rehearsed joke, drawn from his work. He brought a whiff of a smile to those heavily concentrated, almost suspicious faces. Did they really know him? Did they know he had floated twenty feet above the surface of his work for years? No, no, he reassured himself; nobody could know anybody else – thank goodness.

Hamish had been summoned in by Eric Webb a few weeks before the party. Webb was jovial; he told Hamish about the planned festivity and in addition, suggested some dates when Hamish and his wife could join him and his wife for dinner at Webb's home. "It's a great time for you, Dan and you must be feeling good. You're set to enjoy a long and healthy retirement."

"I'm looking forward to it," Hamish said.

"I just want to touch base with you on the Walecka case, you know, the prostitute that was murdered in Southwark?"

Hamish had sensed this might come up. "Sure. We've committed a defendant for trial."

"Uh-huh. I know you've handled this in a very discreet way and that's good. Are you sure that there won't be any… repercussions? You know, the hearing going haywire."

"You mean coming out with nasty stuff about Catesby and his friends?"

Webb could hardly say it. He nodded, opened his mouth on yellow teeth and finally said, "Yes, that's what I mean."

Hamish was irritated at being asked to give Webb this categorical assurance. He moved his head around and tightened his lips equivocally. "It ought to be OK, Eric. But you can never tell. The defendant is facing DNA and forensic evidence. His story, so far, is that he wasn't at the scene."

"Sounds open and shut."

"You know that few cases are open and shut, Eric."

"I do, and if you've got the slightest qualm, we'll drop the charge and let the file gather dust." Webb's narrow, scraggy face was expectant.

Catesby and Co. were *that* important. Hamish thought he'd done his bit for them by deciding to bury Morton's mention of the film. It would have been a tortuous (and perilous) investigation for him if he had decided to pursue it; a pursuit, he was satisfied, he would never conclude. The fog of internal enquiries, reprimands, removals from a case, investigations by the Independent Police Complaints Commission, disciplinary proceedings and dismissals from the service was going to pass him by.

Nevertheless, Hamish *did* have a qualm about the soundness of the prosecution, but on the instant, he decided he wasn't going to reveal it to Webb. He thought it almost certain that come the trial day, Thrussell would admit moving the body from the Dog rather than stick to his story of not being at the scene of the crime and be proved a liar, a guilty liar. And if Thrussell did change his story in this way, that would raise the question: who was at the Dog and what happened? At this moment, after his long service, there was a devil in Hamish, just a little pinpoint of white heat that produced his answer. "I don't have any qualms, Eric."

"Oh, good, good, Dan. You're one man I can take that from. You've always been so damned reliable."

As he was leaving the room with the warmth of Webb's arm around his shoulders, he thought, 'What the hell do I care what happens? It can't touch me.'

Jimmy was pulling pints one night at the Dog & Duck when he received a call from Josie on his mobile. It was about 10pm. At first he didn't recognize her voice, it was so broken. He stuck a finger in his ear to block the noise from the customers and sidled out from behind the bar.

"Jimmy – come at once will you? I'm... I'm in the lavatory... I can't ... I can't..."

He could hear her sobbing. Then he lost the call. He told his boss he had to go out for an hour, an emergency and didn't wait for an answer. He was in a t-shirt and jeans when he went out the doorway and the air was biting. There was no traffic in Butchers' Row. The nearby streets were empty too and wet. He jogged the three or so blocks to a new apartment which Josie had recently acquired, still determined to stay in the neighbourhood. He thought perhaps she was on the needle again. That was the only sense he could make of the call.

When he was in Bleek Street approaching the mansion pile that contained her apartment, he could see a car outside the entrance with the parking lights on; the lobby lights from the building reflected on its glassy surface, a Bentley that in this area was likely to be Catesby's. There was a driver dozing in the car. Jimmy hadn't thought what he could possibly *do*, but he had to intervene. He ran into the lobby. He remembered the elevator was out of order. He sprinted up the dark stairs, three flights and banged on the door. In a few seconds, it was thrown boldly open. Catesby stood fully suited in the lighted space, smoothing his threads of hair.

"Morton! What are you doing snooping around here?"

Jimmy heard a cry inside from Josie. "She called me."

"Rubbish! Clear out you little snipe!" Catesby tried to slam the door.

Jimmy fended off the door and pushed forward with his palms on Catesby's shoulders. "I'm comin' in, mate!"

Catesby stumbled back. "You're interfering in my family affairs, Morton. You'll pay heavily for this!"

Jimmy broke away from him and went into the lounge. It was empty. There was a file of papers on a table with empty liquor glasses, a jug of iced water and a half empty bottle of Scotch. He went through to the main bedroom. Josie was sitting on the bed, barefoot, her dress up to her thighs, her arms hugging around her knees. Her head drooped forward, her hair covered her cheeks.

The front door slammed like a gunshot. Catesby had gone. Jimmy picked up the lace knickers on the floor and dropped them on the bed. He calmly appraised what he saw.

"That's what he used, look." Josie held her head back. A swollen red mark passed around her throat. "I passed out. He raped me."

"Whyn't you pull your gun?"

"Oh, that! I put it in the cupboard. I never had a chance. He flattened me on the bed. He just about knocked me unconscious." She pushed back her hair from her temple and revealed a bruise over her ear. "He was like, mad."

"You should call the cops, *now*, Josie."

"What's the point? Catesby will only have a story like I'm a neurotic druggie which the police will believe without question. He'll include you since you were here and dared to push him around."

"The marks on your throat don't lie to a medico or his semen in you."

"No Jimmy, a complaint would be just like another violation of me by Catesby, *and* the doctors, the police, the lawyers. I couldn't stand it."

"I understand how you feel. But I don't get why you sit down with the man and talk business and have a drink in this private place. He's dangerous. You know that. An' maybe, because you've been arsing him about, he's got it in for you."

"I thought we could have a business meeting. I was wrong. I shouldn't have let him in here. We did the business. We had a drink afterwards. He got up after a while and walked around inspecting the rooms. He joked about taking a fatherly interest. He even went into the bedroom. I don't know whether it was the whisky. He was fired up. He made a lecherous remark about the bed, that I wouldn't have it unless I was fucking somebody. I told him to get out of there but he grabbed me… and dragged me in."

"The guy's a pervert and a killer. He could have killed you. You're sure about what you're doin'? Not calling the cops?"

"Yes," she said, sniffing.

Jimmy thought for a moment about what he could say. It was her prerogative. "You're makin' a big mistake. Skewer the bastard while you have the chance!"

She pressed her face against her raised knees and moved her head negatively.

He waited a while. "There's more in it than that, isn't there? You don't want to screw up the deal you have with Catesby! It's why you wouldn't help with St Edith's. You and Catesby."

She raised a wet, red, swollen face to him. "I've got to live. Why shouldn't I have the money? It's mine. It was my father's!"

"The money's more important than your body. You've been violated. Don't give me crud about lawyers and doctors violatin' you. Do the right thing!"

The room was in silence when her whimpering subsided. He could hear the muted clicking of a distant train. He, too, felt distant from the devastation at his fingertips. He couldn't *do* anything; it was Catesby and Martine in a dance.

"Well, I gotta get back to work, Josie."

"Stay with me, Jimmy."

"Not tonight, Josie." He was thinking maybe not any night. Catesby and Martine Cleland were creatures from another land.

31

Toby drove Jimmy to the airport and waited patiently while he checked in. It was odd to see Toby disenfranchised, standing around waiting. He was a man who was always busy, always in motion. When Jimmy had his boarding card, they stood in the throng near the security entrance. Toby bent over him creating a pocket of lesser noise and said, "I wanted to wish you well, my young friend. Amethyst and I should be going, but I'm stuck..."

"You got good businesses," Jimmy said.

"I'd like to retire. You know, a modest country cottage."

"Sure, a mansion, a Lamborghini and twenty-five acres, I'll bet."

"Let's imbibe one last beaker of coffee," Toby said, leading the way to a café. They tucked themselves in a corner, barricaded behind luggage, with scalding hot cartons in their hands.

"Remember, my lad, if you want to make your fortune, you'll have to sell a lot of mince pies."

"I get the maths. I'll stick to cars, maybe houses."

"Right. You have a gift for mathematics."

"I feel I've just sneaked out before the door closes," Jimmy said. "But I have to come back for a while if I want to emigrate."

"The prison door might slam on you again? Don't worry." Toby laughed, as though it was of little concern.

But the prison door had clanged once on Jimmy,

beginning an unforgettable period of terror. "So, are they goin' to charge Catesby as they should have in the first place?"

"Oh, my God no, Jimmy. Never. That honourable gentleman will remain as he is now, pure as new fallen snow."

"What I don't understand, Toby, is, if Catesby thought he was in the clear with me being arrested, how come he was prepared to let up? Why din't he put the heat on Sneed and Co. in some way to finish me off."

"Ah, Jim-boy, my card was called by that very situation and I played it accordingly."

"What card?"

"A certain graphic film of nocturnal romps trumps all Catesby's cards."

"Y' kept a copy of Garnet's film?"

"Any cautious person would. Catesby must have suspected it. And when he knew, that gentleman absorbed the news without demur, pragmatist that he is. He was quite happy to let Turk and Sneed cook up a charge against anybody else, including the Home Secretary or the Prime Minister, if they so chose."

"What about Catesby's hood. Weren't you afraid he might be visitin'?"

"Not at all. I told Milord Catesby face-to-face – staring into those hot pools that if anything adverse happened to me, the film would go straight to the press without the need for my intervention. I said the film would remain forever confidential otherwise. That was checkmate."

Jimmy shook his head in confusion. "I dunno…"

"You see Jim-boy, we have achieved a fine balance of interests here. Catesby has his film safely snugged away at a fair price. Garnet has been enriched rather than merely recompensed for the tit-touching. I have had my insurance claim against Turk and Sneed duly paid by your release and my own freedom from charges. T&S still have their fine careers, including continued insurance income, and the God of Justice will be propitiated by the conviction of an evil man for a horrible crime."

"But the only other person who could be in the frame, unless they drop the charges, is Kevin – or Tomachek."

"Indeed, so. Alas, poor Kevin. He's already been committed for trial."

"He's a villain, Toby, but he didn't do it."

"That may be so, but nobody in this case is concerned with justice in the abstract or what the actual, literal facts of the murder were. It's about protecting bystanders like Catesby and friends, who are always innocent of wrongdoing, but who might become unluckily involved. It's about protecting your interests and mine and genteel business-ladies like Rita Durbin. It's about getting a man whose face fits. Kevin is clearly a contender and Tomachek too, although Sneed tells me he has an alibi. I think he has insurance."

"What about Hamish? Is he innit too?"

"I'd guess not, but I don't know. Hamish is square. A savvy cop who wants to keep his job. He goes whichever way the wind is blowing."

Jimmy nodded his head slowly, thinking about it. "So, you're goin' to let Kevin go down?"

"Let him? I don't have any say. You and I have our insurance. The Butcher Boys were too bolshie to take out cover, being young and innocent in the ways of the world, or maybe they were barred as bad risks."

"How will Turk get Kevin?"

"DNA evidence, the same way as they were planning to get you. His paws are or will be all over the case."

"Planted."

"Some of it. Fruitful charges can grow from such plants. And Kevin is a very bad lad."

"Surely Catesby's DNA is all over the girl."

"Ah, yes, but only as a customer. Who are we to speculate, my dear James? That fact, if it be a fact, will remain hidden in the recesses of the pathology laboratory," Toby said, long-faced. "Rather concentrate on Kevin in the dock. What a picture! A disagreeable looking rooster. Twelve good and true men and women will recognize him at first sight as a vicious animal. Murder is inscribed on his face and therefore he is well capable of the crime, however smart his mouthpiece. Appearances matter, Jim-boy."

"I'm glad I'm getting out."

"Human beings, though perhaps not all deserve that grand description – shall we say people – are the same everywhere. I beg you, my son, do not have to learn that as a lesson in the southern hemisphere."

"I'll remember, Toby."

"Now what about the charming Josie? I thought she might be going with you. A classy bim if ever there was one."

"Naah. We're friends. I like her, but she ain't my type. She's still, like, tied up with Catesby."

"Like to like, perhaps."

"She was kinda interesting, never more than that."

Jimmy stood up and rested his arm over Toby's shoulders. "Seeya, man," he said and started to tow his drag-bag toward the security entrance.

"Come back soon, my son, and tell me which of those glittering offers of mine you want to accept!"

Jimmy grinned and raised his arm in farewell, swaying on his way as the crowd engulfed him.

32

Shortly after his return to London, Jimmy took a train to the village of Lethbridge in Surrey and walked the leaf-strewn streets in search of Toby's new residence. Toby's occupation of 'the penthouse' had ceased and Jimmy had been invited to visit his home 'in the country'. On the outskirts of the town, he came upon the stone walls which guarded 'The Pines'. After an inaudible exchange on the entry phone, the iron gates swung slowly open to reveal a new Georgian style mansion set in gardens, with neat, low box hedges. Two long and wide lawns like green baize, divided by a drive, reached from the gates to the house. He passed through the gates. He was a few yards from the pillared portico of the house when the tall, white front door opened revealing Amethyst, smiling under a froth of yellow curls and dressed like a rainbow.

"Jimmy!" she called, "Toby's talked so much about you and enjoyed your emails so much..."

Jimmy gave her a hug and stepped inside to notice instantly the contrast between the décor of the wide hall and 'the penthouse'. Here the colours were muted to greys and fawns and the furniture quasi-antique; not, he thought, from the taste of either Amethyst or Toby.

"The traveller returns," Toby said, coming into the hall to greet him. They clasped arms. "You look like a new man, my son." He led Jimmy to a reception room and spread his arms wide. "Fancy, ain't it? Yes, I had a little woman who, at a price, delivered the style."

Jimmy settled in an armchair on a possibly Persian rug, surrounded by what he guessed was imitation period furniture. It was too immaculate to be old. "Y've gone to town here, mate."

Toby busied himself at the liquor cabinet. "Fancy this red?" He held out the bottle for Jimmy to see the Australian label.

Jimmy, remembering the tasting at the Silversmith's Hall, wondered how valid the label was. "Still haven't learned anythin' about wine, Toby, but the Aussies make it good."

Tell me my son whether I'm to be blessed by your presence as the managing director of my private empire. You're very important to me."

"I'm emigrating, Toby. I've made up my mind. It'll be a while before the papers come through. I could do the car sales and auctions in the meantime if it suits you."

"By all means, I'll have you temporary or permanent. I'll swallow the blow, but you must live your life. What have you found Down Under that so appeals?"

"I worked for a guy in Surfers' Paradise selling cars. I told him I could do auctions. He believed me and I just walked into it. I loved it."

"So, you're already an auctioneer? Of course. You're a natural. My loss, Aussie's gain."

"I'm goin' to work for this guy for a while, then, when I can afford it, I'm goin' to get a few cars of my own to sell. Start slowly, build up a stake, like you told me."

"You'll do it, son, I know. Your face is your fortune," Toby said, in a tone mingled slightly with regret. For a while they talked about the transformation of Butchers' Row and some of its inhabitants. Turk had been promoted to Scotland Yard. Harry's Café (Vu Khanh's Café) had closed. Sneed was continuing to collect. Tomachek had moved away to a new flat and a new woman. Rita Durbin remained in business. Ma Thrussell had gone to live with her daughter. And the area was beginning to be dominated by a shining tower of steel and glass. "Fully tenanted in advance I hear and planning a restaurant with a Michelin star chef."

Then Toby said, "By the way, son, those options we've talked about will still be open for the next few months. So, if you change your mind when you get to Oz… You know, things don't always work out."

"Thanks a million for the opportunity, Toby."

"I like a man with a plan. The good burghers of Butchers' Row and environs must sacrifice your just management in favour of Oz. So be it."

"What about the Thrussell trial? What's the story?"

Toby leaned back in his chair and sipped his wine, his eyes misted as he happily recalled the scene. "Yes, that young man's descent was foretold by the numerous acute brains which manipulated this situation. And he went down with a splash that would rival the *Titanic*! Albeit, casting a light spray over the mighty Catesby and friends, standing on a distant shore, but hardly enough to wet their raincoats."

"The dirt came out? Well, a little?"

"Indeed. This is how it was. I ensured myself a front row seat at the Bailey being first in the queue. The drama promised to be more exciting than any show in the West End and so it was. I attended every day for three weeks. The trial was truly educational, James, on the manners and mores of our little community around Butchers' Row; and the wider reaches, where those who have always denied (and will always deny) any wrongdoing, live."

Toby swung his wine glass out to the length of his arm. "First, I give you the most famous courtroom in the land, sombrely panelled, with His Honour in his red dressing gown, disguised as a sheep in his wig; and the serried ranks of counsel, bewigged and cloaked in black; and the registrars and writers with their paraphernalia; and the bobbies in their best uniforms standing straight. There, I have set the scene for you. The tumbril of Justice begins to creak forward, driverless and rudderless. Where on this bleak landscape will it rest?"

"The judge is going to steer it," Jimmy interrupted.

"Oh, certainly, he will try. But the tumbril has to go where the evidence takes it. At this moment, nobody knows where that will be (although some think they do). Chance, my boy, chance.

"There is a flurry amongst the nest of crows while they introduce themselves to the bench and jury. The prosecutor, a learned silk, rises. He tells the short story we already know. Eva's violated body found in the vicinity of Kevin's mother's flat in the building where Eva lived, bearing Kevin's DNA and other incriminating threads. Kevin lied to police about his whereabouts on the night. Simple and conclusive.

Defence counsel rises and announces that Kevin will continue to deny murder but admit that he misled the police. He will say that the truth is that he was paid to remove Eva's body from the Dog by one Rita Durbin, a lady with a whip. That worthy counsel apologises to the court and his learned friends, saying that this news is a result of last minute consultations with Kevin. The absolute truth, he says, is now going to be laid beside the concatenation of alternative stories.

"Consternation! The tumbril of Justice, hardly in motion, has swerved in a direction not wholly unforeseen by some. Has a wheel fallen off? I could not see the physiogs of the crows from where I was sitting, but I fancy they were creased in frowns. The possibility that the noble Catesby and his cronies will have to account for themselves emerges. Turk and Sneed are biting their fingernails and wishing that the murder had remained unsolved. A whole different slew of witnesses will have to practice their elocution to describe the party at the Dog.

"The jury sit to one side, their crumpled faces like two rows of blighted nectarines in the market, some brown, some pink, a few black. What will they make of the play before them? The grid of tensions between the players won't exist for them. They will be sorry for a once pretty girl. They will know Kevin is a hoodlum. One glance will be enough. Catesby will impress them with his clear, not to say angelic certitude; they will feel his electric impulse. Justice is to be done! And I may say, my son, Justice *was* well and truly done in that austere chamber. I almost heard the lady with the scales cry out in pain when it was over.

"Now, look to the dock. There stands Kevin Robert Thrussell, 19, but looking older in a new dark suit, dwarfed by the guardians of the law beside him. The new suit not badly stitched. White shirt. Dark tie. Ginger hair short and slicked down. The Butcher Boys' wardrobe department has done a fair job, but the makeup artist cannot conceal the puffy and mean saturnine features of his face – evidence against him, if anything was. Jim-boy, he was terrified. And he ought to have been. This wasn't like breaking into an old spinster's flat and bashing her round the head to find out where she kept her lolly.

"The prosecutor calls the forensic pathologist to explain poor Eva's fate, which is received in a nauseating silence. This little cameo ramps up a nasty mood. The tumbril is creaking forward, my lad. The indomitable Chief Inspector Daniel Hamish, soft voiced and calm steps into the witness box to give it a shove. Retirement has bestowed a tan on him and a modest smile of ease. He explains that Kevin claimed to have been in Brixton on the night of the crime. Witnesses would show that to be a lie. Yes, Hamish agrees, completely composed, there was a party at the Dog. Yes, forensic and direct evidence shows that Eva was amongst the ladies.

"Hamish, the tactician, is ready for Kevin to change his story; he knows that events at the Dog have to be explained as a harmless little soirée. Yes, the party was for board members of St Edith's Settlement. Yes, there were sexual attractions of a modest nature like pole dancing. My Lord on the bench pipes up: 'We will want to hear what happened at the party from those who were there.

"Rita Durbin, my, what a rock she proves to be. Admittedly a dominatrix, but not required to serve on the night of the crime (she avers). Sees no violence at the party. Eva is alive when she leaves. She knows nothing about Kevin being asked and paid to remove Eva's body. Nothing. Kevin is a liar for implicating her. No mention of paymaster Catesby. Why lose a good client? She said Kevin is a nice lad. She doesn't think he had anything to do with the murder. Yes, she slept with him that night. Gloria Thrussell, prancing like an actress at the Academy Awards, gives monosyllabic confirmation of the innocence of the party. Dearest Garnet is visiting her grandparents in Jamaica and the prosecutor has decided to proceed without her.

"Catesby's lesser men starting with Hassett give evidence like the upstanding and decent fellows they are, rabbits unfairly in the headlights. Catesby brings up the rear to cast a shawl of veracity over their words. His act is most memorable of all. He may seem fierce and nut-brown with his shining forehead, but his elegant tones woo and wed the judge and the jury to his tale. Charitably minded men of business enjoying an evening together and being somewhat startled at the nature of the entertainments on offer. Which, of course, they never participated in. My lord of the bench waves this through as the formality it undoubtedly is. The tumbril is back on track."

Jimmy interrupted. "No mention of drugs. The cops knew all about them."

"Our keeper of the law, Hamish, saw fit not to mention them. It wouldn't have made any difference.

"So, there it is my young friend, an intricately woven quilt of lies and obfuscations. Unfortunately, by changing his story, Kevin faced the need to explain himself – he *had* to step into the witness box. The prosecutor savaged him in his cross-examination – a knight in black prancing in front of the dock, or a sadist whipping a donkey? 'You apprehended this defenceless girl in the dark corridors of the Butcher's Row tenement, *did you not*, etc. etc.' The kid gulps like a goldfish, seemingly unable to understand the implications of the questions, let alone find answers. Obviously, Kevin is a proven liar trying to lie his way out of murder. After retirement, it takes just two hours (including afternoon tea) for the twelve good people to buy the whole nine yards of the trial. I fancy one or two City men would be wiping their brows with their laundered handkerchiefs, changing their underpants and looking forward to a whisky and soda. A sentence of life imprisonment for Kevin to follow in due time. The tumbril grinds to a halt."

Jimmy was shaking his head. "That's wrong, Toby. And it coulda been me."

"It's the way things are, dear boy. Never forget that. We live in a murky pool. A war of all against all. Watch out for predators, son. Have another glass of the Aussie shiraz."

"Did it hit the papers?"

"Oh, yes. But the story only had a 'bit naughty' flavour because nothing could be proved against Catesby and friends. Catesby remains unimpeachably pure. Nobody, not the waiters or the women said anything nasty. And Garnet, remember, has already gone to Jamaica."

"Nobbled? The lot of 'em?"

"Maybe not. Kevin had momentum, as they say, and it didn't take much to push him over the edge."

33

Jimmy walked through the grounds of Southwark Cathedral and under the railway arches. He stopped in his stride when he neared the new Butchers' Row. Ahead of him, out of a wide circle of decaying Victorian buildings like old tombstones, rose the partly finished pinnacle of Catesby's skyscraper. He counted fifty floors and it was aiming to go many floors higher. One side was made partly of glass and threw back the sun's rays. This was to be Catesby's triumph, with the tall cranes nodding respectfully around it.

A viewing platform had been mounted on the lavender fence, now covered with colourful graphics showing the airy and luxurious rooms which had been leased in advance to tenants. He mounted the platform and watched the work for a while. At ground level was a litter of sheds, piles of steel and concrete blocks. The workers on site, with their white helmets, were few and very small. The structure seemed to be climbing of its own efforts. He had a sense that it was another manifestation of Catesby's penis, proclaiming 'Fuck you!' to the world, 'I can do whatever I want!'.

He pictured the scene a year ago. The rear of the old, dark Number 10 in a wilderness of weeds and rubbish. Paul, with his cold hold on the mob of vagrants. Kate Martin, submerged in her files, trying to manage the whole rickety enterprise. He thought about the bonfires he saw from his room and the firewatchers, who had now melted into the dark of doorways and crept under bridges.

He came away from the scene depressed.

Afterwards, Jimmy stopped at the Dog & Duck. The empty bar smelt sour. The publican had his head down over the pipes beneath the counter, mastering the pressure in the beer taps. He looked up when Jimmy blocked the light in the doorway.

"Hiyah, Mark."

"Hey! Jimmy Morton, the tourist. No jobs around here now, Jimmy."

"'Sokay, Mark. I don't need it."

"I've sold out, Jimmy. A nice offer. They're going to redevelop around here. Everybody in the street is buying fur coats and goin' to the races."

"Who's *they?*"

"Same crowd as over the road. Have one on the house."

Jimmy's persistent enquiries enabled him to get an address for Martine Cleland, whom he continued to call Josie. They had exchanged occasional emails, pleasantries, while he was in Australia, but they died out after a few months. Frankly, he got tired of the whining tone of her emails and eventually didn't reply. When Jimmy resumed the correspondence and asked Josie for her street address, saying he was coming home, he received no reply. When he arrived in London, he approached the solicitor whom she once instructed to act for him. He reluctantly told Jimmy that she was a patient at the Tower, a well-known private hospital for treating mental disorders including drug addiction.

He thought about how to approach her and then decided to go directly to the hospital, which was in Wimbledon, without notice. When he arrived, he explained to the sister in charge that he was a friend and Josie was expecting him (which was remotely true). The sister appeared to sum him up. A quiet young man of Josie's age, neatly but casually dressed, with a tanned face and short hair bleached by the sun. He passed the inspection. However, a long pause followed the sister's departure to announce his name. He thumbed through old copies of *Hello* magazine in the waiting room for twenty minutes before the sister reappeared.

"I thought Martine was going to refuse to see you," she said. "I talked to her. It might do her good to see a friend. And she's agreed. I'll just mention she's fragile. She's spent the time since I told her you were here, putting a dress on and makeup and combing her hair. There's an element of pride and self-confidence involved, Mr Morton, so please be gentle."

Jimmy was shown into a room which was almost a suite; it was flooded with sunlight. Martine was not present. The bed did not look like a hospital bed; it had a pale blue counterpane and frilly cushions. The space beside the bed was wide enough to contain two comfortable looking armchairs, a dressing table and a desk. He had an impression of luxurious softness and immaculate cleanliness. No photographs or books and no personal objects decorated the room except a bottle of perfume on the dressing table. A vase of blue flowers was on the desk. The room had an air of bleakness – amid plenty. He realised too late that he had neglected to bring a gift, flowers or chocolates or perfume.

Jimmy stood uncertainly on the threshold, until Josie emerged from the bathroom.

She had lost weight. Her pale dress looked empty, her once shapely legs, what he could see of them, were thin. Her cheeks were hollow, her blue eyes in bruised pits. Even a fashionable cut and careful combing could not disguise her thin and sagging hair. She had powdered carefully over a rash on her cheeks. A diamond ring on the third finger of her right hand caught the sunlight.

"Jimmy Morton. I would never have recognised you!"

"I'm the same guy." He gave her one of his best smiles, the ones that Toby said were charismatic.

"You look like a film star and I bet you know it."

"I wish," he laughed. In fact, he knew he looked different, but not *that* good. A little extra weight, cream chinos, a bright blue shirt under his fleece. A man from a warm climate. He couldn't reciprocate and say Josie looked good because she was alert and she would know. "You haven't been so well."

She threw her hands up in a small gesture of helplessness and sat on the bed. She didn't come close to him. And he couldn't pull her to her feet and kiss her, although he thought perhaps he should. "Sit down," she said, pointing to a chair.

He sat in the floral armchair in the bright room and tried to relax. "You were doin' fine when I left."

She explained that all the business she had to do had overcome her. She thought she was being robbed and she had nobody to turn to, nobody she could trust. "I wished you were still around to help me, Jimmy."

"Whenya gettin outa here?" he asked, warmly.

"Very soon, the doctor says." Her reply seemed to be the impassive repetition of a phrase she had heard from the doctor more than once.

Jimmy thought that 'soon' could be several months. She didn't look fit enough to be discharged at all. She had an edginess, a brittleness.

"I wanted to go abroad with you, Jimmy and maybe if I had..."

"We can't play the 'if only' game, Josie." He spoke gently.

"It was what Catesby did to me, wasn't it, you not wanting me?" she spoke urgently, her eyes widened.

"No. It was bigger than that. What I already told you." He wondered if she was so weak that he would harm her if he talked candidly. And then he did: "It wasn't right to keep quiet about what Catesby did, Josie. Fighting back would have been good for you – win, lose or draw."

"You said it – no 'if onlys'," she said, stoically.

He had a sudden suspicion. "*Did* Catesby come back for more?" He fired the question before he had time to think that it was probably too intimate, the way they were now, and he shouldn't have asked.

Her face reddened and silent tears came. She clasped her hands tightly in her lap.

"So, he did come back. Christ, Josie, the man is a psychopathic killer."

"Some lout was convicted for that," she whispered.

"I already told you, Kevin Thrussell is innocent. He didn't kill Eva. He was stitched up by the cops and Catesby. You *know* Catesby is a rapist, and he coulda killed you that night in your flat, throttled you, but you don't wanna believe he's a killer. This is a man who goes mad when he gets into sex. I don't understand you." What aggravated him was that she didn't seem to appreciate the gravity of what he was saying.

"I don't understand myself. You better go." Her cheeks were wet, her nostrils red and distended.

That was right. He should go. There wasn't any more he could say and, he thought, there was no way now, that he could reach her as a friend, or help her. She was stained by Catesby's shadow. He was dumbfounded and sickened by the continued connection. "You need to dump Catesby for your own good, Josie."

"Are you going back to Australia?"

"When I get the papers… any day."

"Couldn't I come with you? Not as a lover. I know you don't want me. Just a friend… please."

"I'm emigrating, Josie. I'm gone. For good."

"I know, but…"

He didn't feel she was even a friend. She was obtuse about Catesby; that was like a concrete wall separating them. There was a long pause in the room. The sun beat in. He could feel the sweat on his temples. She looked like a little bundle of sticks. She was wringing her hands. Her eyes were red and desperate. He said mildly, almost hopelessly, "No, Josie. You can do better than me. A different kinda guy. You need to get well and axe Catesby."

"Axe him? Yes, he deserves it…" She gave a quick, humourless laugh. "But why can't I come, Jimmy? Why, why, why?"

Her shrieking voice unsettled him again. He spoke quickly, "Because I want to brush off all the Catesby shit!"

"So do I. I truly do. And if you and I were to go to Australia…"

"No. Josie…" He thought whether he should explain. He was feeling increasingly remote from her as they talked. He could say that he realised she was deeply involved with Catesby and that couldn't be ended overnight; that was the tactful explanation.

"Why?" she demanded.

Her screech was like a razor on his nerves. "Because you're part of it. The shit!" That was the truth. She had become repulsive.

She screamed and leaped toward him. "You should never have come here, never!"

He stood up quickly. She raised her arm and he saw

the flash of surgical scissors in her fist. He fell back as they collided. He was conscious of the door opening behind him. With both hands he baffled the blows she aimed at him. He felt the pain of the scissors in both palms. Strong hands grabbed him from the rear. Josie, howling, was encircled by two female nurses and pushed back tenderly on the bed. He was hustled from the room into an adjoining vacant bedroom by a male nurse, staunching the blood running from his hands with a towel. "Sit down Mr Morton and we'll attend to your cuts."

He boarded the Underground at Wimbledon station with two bandaged fists. The sister had rebuked him for upsetting Josie. "You're the well person, Mr Morton, and you are the one who had to exercise self-control. As for the wounds on your hands, you brought them on yourself!" She said how harmful it would be for Josie if he complained about the incident. He assured her he would not complain or visit again without a prior arrangement. The sister, a blunt Yorkshirewoman, told him not to come again. He apologised for the trouble he had caused.

As the returning train passed through Putney Bridge station his palms were throbbing. He was considering whether he should have visited Josie at all. Kindness to a friend was a motive. He wasn't clear what he could do to help her, but he had hoped to find that out. Or was it dumb of him not to realise that the one thing she would want, was the one thing he *could* do, but wouldn't – take her to Australia? She was right. He should never have visited.

His curiosity was admittedly also a motive. He had always been curious about her, a person from another kind of life. Josie was, in many ways, unknowingly central to Eva's murder. He had seen Catesby through her eyes, a unique view of an evil man. He could now see that her arrival at Butchers' Row, at the time of Eva's murder, signalled the ruin of St Edith's Settlement and the obliteration of its identity.

He knew that most people would consider Catesby's skyscraper as merely a financial transaction, market forces reallocating valuable land, a normal phenomenon. And an enhancement of the area. He appreciated that anybody could look at St Edith's as a failed charity, only kept alive by the skills of its selfless directors – and its time had come. Some few cynics might want to say that St Edith's penny pinching masters used it to gratify a perverse and ignoble wish to cleanse themselves. Jimmy didn't view the advent of Catesby and the destruction of St Edith's in any of those ways. He saw St Edith's simply, doing a useful job as it scraped along, sheltering some of the homeless, protecting a few battered women and providing cups of tea for lonely people. In contrast, he regarded Catesby as a *force* with a thrust and velocity which cast these efforts, and other people, aside, including Josie. He performed clever feats, lauded by City professionals, making his fortune and the fortunes of his friends, a malign and somehow protected force, that gorged on money and on sex.

By the time the train reached Earl's Court, he was beginning to think again about whether he could do anything to try to save Kevin. In the years that they had lived together uneasily in Ma Thrussell's flat, he had begun to feel sorry for Kevin, despite the poverty of their similar positions. They had both had about the same amount of formal schooling, dwindling away before college level with suspensions and truant absences. Their shared view of schooling at that time was that it was a burden unreasonably imposed by adults, to be shed as soon as possible; real life was something else. But Jimmy, who could never tolerate the necessary schoolroom constraints, at least had a thirst to learn and a natural curiosity. Kevin had no such urges. He was uncritically susceptible to peer group influence, while Jimmy was suspicious of it. Kevin's membership of the Butchers Boys gang was accepted by him as an honour. As a result, he had invested himself with the persona of a hard man which Jimmy thought was childish. Kevin was playing tough, except that in practice it wasn't playing; it was brutal. Kevin didn't seem to have learned from experience in Jimmy's opinion; it was a terrible flaw, a kind of blindness.

Jimmy started to think that perhaps he held the key to Kevin's prison cell. He was present on the night of the killing with Kevin at Butchers' Row. He knew about the party. He had talked to Gloria and Garnet. He knew about the film, but he believed that the copy of it, which Toby had, could not be available to him without trouble for Toby. Could Garnet ever be brought back from Jamaica for a retrial? And there were so many things he had heard from Toby which pointed to Catesby's guilt but couldn't be mentioned publicly because of his own relationship with Toby. Toby was a friend and mentor who would get into serious trouble if he talked. And much of what he knew was just hearsay anyway. Maybe he didn't hold the key; all he had was the knowledge that Catesby had murdered Eva and Kevin was innocent. And that wasn't enough.

Assuming he was going to try to save Kevin, how would he start? He might write a full statement for the police or the newspapers. He might take legal advice. He appreciated that whatever he did would entail the delay of months, raise questions about his own motives and invoke the powerful and unseen forces of opposition that Toby had made him aware of in the course of the case. And it would spell ruin for Toby, perhaps death.

By the time the Tube train had reached Westminster, where he changed for London Bridge, he had concluded that the odds were heavily against him being able to save Kevin. As Toby had said, 'Alas, poor Kevin.'

The same sense of wanting to help and believing he could, which took Jimmy to see Josie, led him to want to visit Kevin in Belmarsh high security prison. He felt guilty with the weight of his knowledge and the inability to use it. He had no idea how to find Betty Thrussell or Gloria now that the Butchers' Row tenement had been demolished, but he obtained the approximate address of Gloria's council house from an acquaintance at the Dog & Duck. A few enquiries in the neighbourhood found him the property. It was one of a newly built, low level block, with a small, fenced front garden, full of tall weeds. About one in five of the front gardens in the row was cultivated; the rest were accumulating wind-blown newspapers and plastic bottles. Despite the imaginative architecture of the units, there was an air of gloom about the block. Gloria in a stained t-shirt and tousled hair answered his knock, the sound of children yelling behind her.

"Oh, it's you." Gloria's pasty face clouded over.

"I wanted to see you. Talk about Kevin."

"You're lookin' very pretty, mister bigtime world traveller." She blocked the door ajar. She wasn't going to invite him inside.

"Wossup up with you, Gloria?"

"*Talk* about Kevin? Wots to talk about? Kevin's doing time, ain't he? An' you dobbed him innit with the cops."

"No way. How could I do that? I wasn't anywhere near

the trial. I wasn't even in the country for most of it."

"Yeah, you scarpered, after you'd put the cops on Kevin's tail."

"I didn't scarper. I couldn't have gone if the cops had wanted me."

"You was under arrest yourself. You was in pokey for a week. Howja get outta that?" Jimmy searched for an answer, shaking his head in denial. "They didn't have evidence against me. Nothin'."

"I'll tell you how you got out – by pissin on Kevin." Gloria's squarky voice seemed very loud in the quiet street.

He faced a woman who had drawn herself up like a sentinel and clamped her wide mouth so that it showed only a thin line of pale lip. "Not true, Gloria." He backed away.

"You ain't welcome here, Jimmy, not ever!"

Jimmy knew now that he was likely to get a bad reception from Kevin, but he was determined to see him. He obtained permission in advance to visit Belmarsh, hired a car and drove down the south bank of the Thames to Woolwich. It was a fine day and he stopped for scrambled eggs on toast at an empty café just out of the town. He presented himself on time for his afternoon visit.

He had an uneasy feeling as he approached the high walls. He had not forgotten the desperation of his own imprisonment. Inside, the identity checks, searches and security barriers were formidable and seemed to take hours. He was processed like a commodity by men who did not smile. Eventually, he was directed to a misty window of armoured glass. Resting on the ledge before it was a telephone speaker-receiver on a cord. He waited, looking into the empty space behind the glass. Kevin, roughly shaven and dressed was brought in by a guard and seated. His carrot hair had been shaved. His cheeks were flushed and lined. He looked like a user to Jimmy. He seemed to have aged, to have acquired a new degree of cold masculinity. Arrest, remand, trial, sentence and prison. How would an innocent man make this horrifying descent? Jimmy knew a little from his own experience. It was a long drawn out agony, an agony which would go on for Kevin's life, even for a man like him with iron insensitivity.

Kevin's red eyes appraised him. "So, you've come. Gloria said you might. Come to gloat, hey? Show off your suntan. You cunt!"

"I came because I know you're innocent but there isn't anythin' I can do. I've thought hard about it, but there isn't anythin'. I wanted you at least to know that."

"Yeah, I'm innocent, as you knew when you ratted on me."

"If I ratted on you, the cops woulda nailed me as a witness against you. The reason they didn't want me as a witness, was cos they knew *I said you was innocent*."

"How come you knew so much?"

"I helped clean up at the Dog & Duck an' I talked to the girls who were at the party. What I know isn't evidence. It's just fuckin' common sense." He was too cautious to mention the video.

"Mr Smartarse!"

"No, Kevin. The cops wanted somebody to hang this on. They could never skewer Arnold Catesby. They coulda got evidence against him, but he's too big to touch. They tried me first. Then they found I was at the shelter all the time. So they grabbed you.

"So it's all about wicked coppers?" Kevin said, with derisive bitterness.

"Nah. Don'tcha geddit? It's about people who are too big to touch. We're just maggots in their game."

Kevin was silent for a moment. His eyes dropped down. Then he said, "Yeah, yeah, yeah," quietly. He swung away and stood up. The guard, who was standing at the back of the room, moved forward, a baton in his hand.

As Jimmy came away from the window, he thought Kevin was seeing and feeling the crushing immovability of the vice that was holding him.

Four months later, Jimmy's emigration papers had been approved and he was booked on a flight from Heathrow to Sydney. He was expecting Toby might want to see him off. He had said his goodbyes to the acquaintances who were still around the Butchers' Row area. He was pleased when Toby loomed out of the crowd with a hearty shout. "You ain't got too much luggage, son!"

"I don't need it where I'm goin'."

"And the moolah?"

"Enough, Toby."

"Never enough. Here's a donation from St Bernard's," Toby said, producing a cheque.

Jimmy scowled at the cheque. "That's one hell of a lot of dough." The cheque was for £10,000. "You shouldn't do this, Toby."

"What did I tell you, Jimmy? Dogs. Everybody loves them. Dogginess is not going to stop. St Bernard's will prosper for a long time to come… Take Amethyst and me out to dinner when you touch down here again."

His expression became intimate and he leaned close to Jimmy, opening his eyes wide and said in a low, amused, questioning voice: "One interesting little bit of news in the papers, my boy. Our forthcoming leader, Milord Sir Arnold

Catesby, Knight of the Realm, is tucked up in Chelsea Westminster Hospital with a gunshot wound. Nothing serious. The police say they are satisfied that a licensed firearm was accidentally discharged on a family occasion."